Dynami

Winging It

Books in this series so far:

Deliciously Deceased

Delectably Departed

Dynamically Dead

Published in 2018 by Emma L Beal

Copyright © EmmaLBeal2018

Cover Design: *Paul Beal MBIE*

Dedicated to: *Deborah (Debs) Broome MBIE / Dip F.D (aka – Dendra)*

Emma L Beal has asserted her right to be identified as the author of this work in accordance with the Copyright, Designs and Patents Act 1988.

All rights reserved. No part of this publication may be reproduced, stored in a retrieval system, or transmitted in any form or by any means, electrical, mechanical, photocopying, recording or otherwise without the prior permission of the copyright owner.

All characters appearing in this work are fictitious. Any resemblance to real persons, living or dead is purely coincidental.

Darkness envelops her as she runs as fast as her legs and lungs will allow.

Her breathing becomes jagged as she screams out for her to stop, oh why won't she stop?

Brambles catch in her hair trying to slow her progress, but she does not stop. She does not feel the pain as her hair is ripped from the roots, she does not feel the blood as the sharp thorns tear at her arms, and she does not feel the blisters already forming and bursting open upon her bare shredded feet.

All she needs is for her to stop.

Come away from there! She screeches in her mind, her voice no longer able to make sound.

Exhausted she falls to her hands and knees, her blood and tears spill onto the muddy ground beneath her, her breathing is laboured as she tries to move forward again, clawing at the ground, praying for help, praying for anything.

She cannot move, her lungs are done, and her body is weak.

She is too late.

Chapter One

Speed dating? Is Celestia for real?
Like anybody would for even a nano second look at me and believe that I needed help in the dating department. *Hardly!*
So, L.U.V is under attack, let me explain.
L.U.V has recently opened in the heart of Leeds City Centre and is now *the* place to be if you are a little down on your luck in the dating department. Unfortunately for the ladies of Leeds, it is not only Mr Right they need to look out for, it is also Mr Wrong. *(Assuming of course that this is all down to a man).* You see, these poor love forlorn desperados are being taken, picked off one by one, swept away in a cloud of mystery, and not even in a good way. *Poor schmucks!* And now I must go under cover and try to find out who is doing this, and why.
My name is Tiffany Delamarre; I am dead and very much in demand.
You see I was murdered not so long ago by some loser geek called Gemma, to cut a long story short she was a jealous weirdo who hated me because I'm rich and beautiful. Okay, well maybe there is a little bit more to it than that. She hated me because as well as being rich and beautiful I was a complete and utter bitch when I was alive. I bullied one of her other friends mercilessly and for that I paid the ultimate price, I paid with my life.
She killed me and dumped my body outside of Oxfam, seriously! Oxfam! She then proceeded to kill or attempt to kill each of my so called friends in turn until myself and

my yummylicious Guardian Angel / Boyfriend Daniel Fox stopped her.

So this is what I do now, I reside in Heaven and I solve mysteries so that my brain doesn't turn into decomposed mush. Damien Kernick would know all about that if it were ever to happen, he's the embalmer guy that I met whilst trying to solve my own murder, good looking but seriously odd. Oh and just to point out that I did not mean that his brain is decomposed mush, that would just be plain rude. I had initially believed that Damien was the killer, based purely on his general creepiness and the fact that he hangs around with dead bodies all day, but I was wrong.

Celestia is the queen bee of Heaven, what she says goes, though I have pushed this on more than one occasion, much to her dismay. She can be stern and she can be a real pain, but deep down she means well... I think.

My other friends in Heaven are Tracey and Victoria, they are the closest *true* friends that I have ever had and they mean a lot to me. Tracey helped me solve a case a little while back and our friendship was firmly cemented from then. Victoria unfortunately was not so lucky, her daughter was killed and in her grief she committed suicide. I did manage to find out who did it *(the stupid husband),* and she was reunited with her little girl, but still, it sucks to be dead.

Now here I am once more, trying to play a part that I just do not fit into.

Tiffany Delamarre single? Tiffany Delamarre desperate? *Not even close*!

Three girls have been kidnapped from this venue, there has been no contact from the kidnappers, no ransom demand,

no body parts through the post – *thank god*, and no clues up to press as to where they could be or who could have taken them.
Jemma Daines, Freya Scopes and Amanda Farthing have literally just vanished.

Looking through the haze of smoky air *(the fabricated party kind, not cigarettes)* I stifle a groan as I take in the spectacle before me. Never ever in all of my life have I seen such desperation. The atmosphere positively reeks of it. With its low lights, squishy love seats and gold chandeliers, the room could not look more gaudy or seedy if it tried.
Women rush to tables, each eager to find their perfect match this evening, each longing to fulfil some deep routed desire inside of themselves that only this farcical event can produce.
Men straighten ties, flatten down toupees and straighten spectacles as they hungrily stalk their prey with their eyes. Women fluff up hair and reapply lipstick, seductively glancing around the room, making only the right amount of eye contact, just enough to entice but not enough to immediately commit. It is like watching a documentary on the mating rituals of some docile beast.
Surely the possibility of meeting the man or woman of your dreams does not lie within this darkened seedy room? Stifling a groan I make my way towards the only table left, this is so not my idea of a pleasant evening. As the bell tinkles merrily I hold my breath and wait for loser number one to sit before me.

... 'So yeah, I love my trains. I suppose it's just the sheer excellence of the engineering, not to mention the...'
I drown him out and cover my yawn with my Martini glass, could a person actually be bored to death? This is only round one and if I weren't already dead then I would put some serious consideration into committing suicide. What an absolute bore!
'Do you have an interest in trains?' he asks me excitedly.
'No.' I respond abruptly, sure it's rude, but for crying out loud how much of a conversation can you have on trains! 'I have this little thing...' I smile, '...it's called a life.'
He doesn't wait for the bell to chime signalling the end of our brief and yet seemingly long meeting, he heads directly for the bar and orders another drink whilst scowling at me menacingly.

Rounds five and six pass in a blur of even more tedious interaction and sexual innuendo, and I can't help but wonder why I am here. I have not seen anything that could be described as out of the ordinary. Creepy and pathetic yes, but a kidnapping about to take place absolutely not!
Maybe I am missing something, maybe I should be speaking to the women and not the men. Would it be classed as a little late in proceedings to momentarily change my sexual orientation?
Signalling the waiter I order another Martini and Lemonade and turn my attention to the ladies in the room. Tonight one of them could be going away with a total nutjob and I have absolutely no idea which one it is going to be.
There are twenty two women, myself included and twenty two men, each with their own personal agenda, I however

have taken myself out of proceedings, there is no way that I am sitting through another sixteen rounds of gouge your eyes out tedium.

There are eleven brunettes, four blondes, four wannabe blondes, two red heads and a rather striking woman with shocking blue hair and bright red lips. I immediately cross the latter off of my mental list; surely her disappearing would be way too noticeable.

The men range from basic looks to pretty average.

Not one of them looks like a kidnapper or a psychopath, but to be fair neither did Peter Sutcliffe and just look at the devastation he caused.

Slipping elegantly onto a bar stool I sip my Martini and say hello to the blue haired wonder sitting beside me. It looks like she too has given up with this strange lot. She eyes me suspiciously, should I maybe tell her that I'm heterosexual and so totally not coming onto her.

'Hi' she smiles back after a moment, question answered. 'You having a good time?'

'Not really.' I answer truthfully, 'To be honest this isn't my cup of tea, but my friends thought maybe it was time to date again.' I lie smoothly and can instantly tell that she is taken in.

'Oh dear, what happened.' she asks softly. 'If you don't mind my asking of course?'

I lie again, 'My fiancé ran away with another woman the night before our wedding, it was awful, just awful.' I sigh dramatically.

'Well that's just terrible.' she soothes, 'but... at least you now know what kind of man he is before you fully commit yourself to him.'

'I suppose.' I let my comment linger a moment before I

delve straight into what I really want to know. 'Don't you feel a little paranoid being here?'

'Paranoid?' she looks at me quizzically, 'Oh, do you mean because of my blue hair?'

'Well no, not exactly. I mean because of all of the women that keep disappearing from here. Doesn't it put you on edge? It certainly makes me feel a little apprehensive.'

She laughs and totally evades my question. 'Look, let me get you another drink and then you can tell me all about those fabulous eyes!'

Her comment throws me and I find myself backing away from her, I had forgotten that I no longer wear my blue contact lens to cover my one green eye, Daniel told me that I am beautiful without it, and I believe him. I have no problem now with my heterochromia, but it sure does throw me when I've forgotten all about it and someone brings it up.

'Now now, don't be embarrassed about it.' She laughs, 'you look amazing.'

'I'm not embarrassed!'

'Okay.' she replies simply, 'but you must tell me all about it. Is there only you in the family that has it? Are you likely to pass it along to your children?' She quizzes me none stop and I feel anger building deep within me.

'It is not a disease!' I shout, 'It is perfectly normal and perfectly fine!'

She places her hand on my arm and I shrug it off with obvious annoyance, 'I didn't mean to offend you, I'm just interested that's all. I think you are perfect, and isn't perfect what we all long to be?' Her voice is wispy, almost dreamlike as she gazes off into the distance.

Leaving her staring at god knows what I make my way

across the room and pray that the next person I speak to is not a loon. Something in me however cannot stop thinking about the way she said the word 'perfect', like it was a dream, a goal, something that she aspires desperately to be, which is crazy considering how beautiful she is.

She should take it from me, striving to be perfect is not all that it is cracked up to be.

Glancing at my watch I see that the last few hours have passed rather quickly. The bell rings again signalling that round eleven will commence after a short refreshment break and I take this as my opportunity to round up a few ladies. The blue haired woman is still by the bar, she does not seem to want to interact with the other women in the room, she does however catch me watching her and turns away quickly to speak into her mobile phone, whilst making her way towards to exit. Maybe she has had enough; maybe she wants to leave here under her own steam and not by some crazed kidnapper.

Smoothly joining the small group of women that have gathered by the buffet table I introduce myself and listen intently to their conversation.

'It is awful, but what can you do? If you listened to every news story you'd never leave the house would you.' Begins a blonde wannabe.

'True, true. My sister said not to come tonight, but... here I am.' laughs a red haired woman.

'I doubt any of the guys here would even have it in them to kidnap a woman, they don't even have it in them to restrain from looking at our boobs at every given second. Infants.'

'Do you think the kidnapper is not here then?' I ask innocently.

'Nah, the cops are all over the place looking for this

clown, it would be stupid to rock up here again so soon after the last girl.'

Everybody sighs in relief, though I do not believe that any of them were actually worried to begin with. 'Why do you suppose he takes them?' I ask again, eager to not let the subject change.

'Well the papers are saying it's because he has some weird fascination with dolls, on account of all of the women so far have been blonde, skinny and beautiful.' She eyeballs me, 'Hey you should be careful, you seem to be giving off a major Barbie vibe right now.'

I laugh in response to her silly comment but silently thank her for reading the newspaper and finally giving me some kind of a lead.

A man that kidnaps women because they look like dolls? What exactly is he doing with them after he takes them away from here?

What does one do with a doll? Why you play with it of course.

The thought sends shivers down my spine, just what kind of playing is he doing?

Walking away from the women and the club I silently name this man 'The Collector' on account of my not knowing whether the women are still alive and well and are being used as part of some bizarre doll display, or if they are dead and still being used as part of some bizarre doll display.

'The Collector'. Where are you hiding?

Chapter Two

'There was nobody there of interest *at all*?' Celestia is in her usual demanding mood, and for the life of me I just cannot seem to get her to understand that kidnappers do not walk around with signs on their backs declaring who they are and what their intentions are. 'Well somebody must have looked out of place' She continues, totally oblivious to my eye rolling and under my breath mutterings.

'Nobody looked out of place, but me! I mean seriously Celestia like I'd pass as some loser that needs help finding a man.' I snort unattractively and Daniel raises one eyebrow in my direction. 'Okay, okay. Other than the blue haired crazy lady and the countless number of weirdo's that I had to chat up... *boring*... there wasn't anybody in particular that screamed out serial kidnapper. Though...' I pause for dramatic effect then quickly hurry up as I see Celestia take one of her 'ready to rant' breaths, 'I do have a theory.'

If looks could knock you down like an elephant charging at you full speed, then the glaringly obvious look of *'here we go again'* that passes between Daniel and Celestia would have floored me. *Doubtful fools*.

'I wait with bated breath.' whispers Celestia to Daniel, Daniel at least has the courtesy of hiding his snigger behind a rather overdramatic yawn.

'I am here you know! I can hear you. I mean seriously, what is your problem with me... *again*?'

She eyeballs me in the only way that Celestia can, 'The

problem is that women are disappearing willy nilly and you have one of your theories, which I am inclined to believe will be yet another hair brained scheme that will leave us exactly nowhere.'

I swear she actually wiggled her fingers in the air when she said *theories*, who even does that! 'Wow, I just don't think I quite got how blunt you were trying to be there!' I snap viciously, 'I'll tell you what, I will keep my *theories...*' Little bit of finger wiggling of my own. '...to myself and fill you in when you are less...shall we say... temperamental?'

She rises from her chair like an angry demon, her face distorted and red, hair wild, arms flailing. Pushing herself over the desk she lunges for me, hands around my throat, choking the death out of me...

'Tiff! Are you even listening?' Daniels voice has me back in the room. 'Let's go.'

'Sorry, I drifted off there.' I mutter. Bloody hell, now I'm day dreaming about the woman! What the hell is wrong with me?

Daniel is heading for the door and I see that Celestia has once again buried herself under the mountain of paperwork that has piled up on her desk. Why do dead people require so many forms I wonder to myself.

We have been dismissed. *Charming.*

'Thank you ever *soooo* much for sticking up for me back there, I have absolutely no doubts whatsoever now that you have my back.' I smile at Daniel. 'Thanks, really.'

'Aaaw c'mon honey, you saw how she was in there, there's clearly something going on that's she's not telling us.' He puts his arm around my shoulders and as much as I want to shrug it off out of sheer childishness I do not, purely because it feels so nice.

'Celestia always has something going on, and it's normally always directed at yours truly.'

'You have to admit though, that was pretty rude even for her.'

'I am at a point now Daniel where nothing that she does surprises me anymore. She didn't even want to hear my theory on the kidnappings.' I sulk.

Pulling me closer and kissing my forehead Daniel steers me in the direction of the restaurant, 'Well tell me whilst I eat my body weight in eggs and bacon, I'm starved.'

Daniel I have noticed really enjoys his food, and I mean *really* enjoys it. You wouldn't think so from how lean his body is, but it seems to me that he is always eating.

I remember once reading an article that declared the way to a man's heart is through his stomach. I remember laughing at the absurdity of it, but now I see what they mean.

Poor unfortunate Daniel Fox however has yet to learn that I am unlikely to be any kind of domestic goddess. I truly do not think that I could even fry an egg. I wonder if I should point this out before we are married?

'...and so it makes perfect sense that the kidnapper has some kind of doll fetish and that is why there have been no bodies discovered, because he is keeping them like trophies, collecting them.'

I have filled Daniel in on my theory of 'The Collector' and he did not interrupt once. That may be because his face was constantly being filled with masticated pig, but still I have my theory out there and I feel a little bit better for it.

'So let me get this straight.' He begins, wiping his mouth of egg yolk, 'The women that have been kidnapped have all been blonde, slim and attractive? Much like a Barbie doll? That's quite a leap Tiff, maybe he just prefers blondes.'

'I understand that Daniel I'm not retarded, but the newspapers made the initial leap to the idea, and the more I think about it the more it makes sense. If he has some kind of fixation with beautiful blonde women, like maybe he felt he wasn't good enough for them, then surely he would strike out at them in anger, killing them. And there have been no bodies found... anywhere.'

'Maybe he's just hidden them really well and we have yet to discover them? I hope that it is your theory Tiff I really do; at least that way we have a slim chance that these women are still alive. What do you want to do next? Any ideas?'

'Well... I thought it would be a good idea to talk to the people that were at L.U.V last night, away from the seedy atmosphere and desperation. Get them when they aren't all dolled up *looking for love.*' I laugh.

'You really despise those kinds of places don't you? Some folk just need a helping hand in that department, they can't all be as fortunate as you and I.'

'I just feel that it could be done in a less desperate fashion that's all.'

Waving a dismissive hand and pushing his now empty plate away he rubs his full stomach and asks who is first on my list to question.

I grimace, for number one is creepy train man.

Chapter Three

'I am *not* going in there with my Louboutins.' I screech as we pull up outside of creepy train man's house. 'Not a chance in Hell.'

'Mmm don't think you should be making references about going to Hell, do you honey?'

'Blah blah blah.' I mutter, 'It was a brief visit and Lucifer was incredibly pleasant.'

'Are you actually...'

'Shhh I am just teasing you.' I smile, 'I promise never ever to go to Hell again, satisfied?'

He groans, 'I'd be more satisfied if you hadn't gone in the first place.'

'Can we not go into this right now, please? There are more serious issues at hand, like my shoes.' I wriggle my feet in his direction and he looks totally nonplussed.

'They're just shoes Tiff.'

'Just shoes! Just shoes! I will have you know...'

'Yeah yeah they cost a billion quid and you'll just die again if they get ruined, heard it a million times Tiff and I say it again, they are just shoes.'

'I never said that they cost one billion pounds, you just have no idea about fashion, if you...'

'Are we going in or not?' He interrupts, 'There's some wellies in the boot if you're that concerned.' He laughs.

Scowling I slam the door of the car and take in the creepy sight before me.

The house is quite a size and I am sure if somebody of a less frightening demeanour were to own it, it would be rather pleasant. Unfortunately that is not the case here and the house has a nightmarish appearance instead.

With its large black metal gates, long sweeping driveway and stairs leading up to the front door you could quite easily imagine that it looks quite decadent. But when you add in the dying lawn, skeletal trees, faded paintwork on the bricks and the huge dirty windows overlooking the whole front of the property it is easy to imagine that you are being observed, and not in a friendly way.

Looking back for Daniel I see him in a heated conversation with a traffic warden and stifle a groan of annoyance. I wonder if traffic wardens have their own special place in Hell?

'You go on up honey.' He calls to me, 'I'm gonna have to move the car, this gentleman is being totally unreasonable.'

I wonder what would happen if Daniel were to receive a parking ticket? What would the traffic warden's superiors say when they see that the ticketed person is in fact deceased?

Taking a deep breath I push open the creaky gates and make my way towards the front entrance. I swear to God if the front door creaks as well I am so out of here!

Raising my hand tentatively towards the door knocker I hold my breath and...

'I knew it was you.' The nerdy voice reverberates around my eardrums and I take a steadying breath as I behold the spectacle before me. Creepy train man is wearing a neon green shellsuit and a bumbag. Let me just repeat that.

A NEON GREEN SHELLSUIT AND A BUMBAG! Now I know that once upon a time in a decade a long long time ago these were the height of fashion... but today...

right now... May 2018... *NO*!

'Hi, I erm... well the thing is...' I am lost for words. I can't question this man while he's leering at me like I'm the best thing he's seen in like, forever. I mean to be fair I totally am, but...

'I had a feeling about you.' he winks, 'I knew we had a connection. I can understand why you were so standoffish with me, after all, those places can be totally tense. I've been to a few myself so I'm used to it, but I could see that you were out of your depth. So I forgive you for the way you spoke to me, I knew in the end it was all just nerves. Oh I am so glad that you came looking for me. Somehow I knew that you would.' He laughs and I cringe deep inside my soul.

'Okaaay! Listen Mr...'

'See we didn't even get to exchange names you were that scared, poor little mite. Call me Albert, please. And you are?'

'Totally at a loss of what to say to you. Look Albert, there is a very clear misunderstanding here, you see I wasn't in that place looking for somebody, I was there...'

'Looking for The One! Me too! And aren't we just so lucky to have found one another amidst all of those other people looking for true love.'

'No. Seriously, just no.'

'I can see that you are still a little nervous about all of this, well when true love strikes it's a fairly big jolt to the system... much like when trains...'

'Oh. My. God. Will you please just stop!'

'Cars parked honey, you get what you needed?' Daniel thankfully comes up the stairs behind me and I watch him eyeball Albert with suspicion. 'Everything okay?'

'So you have two people on the go do you?!' Albert is suddenly very angry and I take a step back. 'She's playing you pal.' He directs at Daniel. 'Came here to declare her love for me and now look, wasn't expecting you to turn up was she?' He snarls.

'We came together actually. What exactly is the problem here?'

'Oh like that is it!' Albert thunders, 'well let me tell you that I am NOT into that kinky stuff, you people disgust me!' Turning on his heel with a dramatic shake of his head he flounces back into the creepy house and slams the door.

'What the hell was that?' Laughs Daniel completely bemused by the last few minutes.

'That dear Daniel was Albert, aka creepy train man, totally not our kidnapper.'

The rest of the day passes in a blur as we continue to question the remaining twenty one men, twenty one women, and the event organiser. Not one of them had anything particularly helpful to say.

The event organiser was a strange woman called Lizzie Carver, our conversation after the initial introductions went like this:

Lizzie: Every person in this world has a perfect love match out there for them and it is my calling to bring those two lost souls together.

Me: So you are saying that even rapists and serial killers have a perfect love match? That they deserve affection despite what they have done?

Lizzie: I do not decide who should be loved and who of us should be left unloved, just that there is somebody out there for us all.

Me: You would help those kinds of monsters find love though?
Lizzie: If I was called upon to do so, then yes, I suppose that I would. I didn't choose my calling, it chose me.
Me: How so?
Lizzie: One day I woke feeling so so unhappy, I was alone, single, lonely. Something just happened, a thought, a little seedling of an idea. I just knew instantly that I could do good.
Me: And all of this came about from waking up sad?
Lizzie: You may jest, but love is an important thing, it moves us all in a profound way.
Me: Have you ever noticed anything unusual happening at any of these events? Has anything ever gotten out of control?
Lizzie: In what way? Each individual that attends these special evenings are only there for peace and love, why would anything get out of control?
Me: Are you aware that recently three young women have been taken from evenings at L.U.V without their consent and they have not been seen again?
Lizzie: Why of course, but not necessarily from my nights.
Me: What makes you say that?
Lizzie: I would know, I would feel it deep within my heart if anybody were to be hurt.
Me: Is that so? Well it's been proven that the girls were taken from *your nights* so I guess your soul radar must be a little off.
Lizzie: I hear what you are saying but I disagree.
Daniel: Do these things ever last though, other than the initial 'getting together' if you know what I mean. *Daniel actually winked at this point.*

Lizzie: I know perfectly well what you mean Mr Fox and I will not answer your perverse question. Good day to you both.

And that was the end of that. *Well done Daniel.*

The only person remaining on the list to see is the blue haired woman, I am doubtful that she will know anything and I am also doubtful that she has ever been a target for the kidnapper on account of her rather bold appearance. But still, she is the last person on the list and I would like to be able to say that we questioned everybody that has been to L.U.V recently.

I am anxious about seeing her again, I hope that her weird fixation with my eyes has passed and she does not turn the questioning around to me again.

I am totally fine about my eyes now. Sure it took a lot of looking at, and dealing with some raw emotions based around my heterochromia, but I did it. I suppose I just prefer not to talk about it. I just hope that the blue haired woman leaves me be.

Chapter Four

Blue haired woman lives in an ordinary house, in an ordinary street. No creepy gates or dying grass, no freaky windows and no decaying trees. I let out a sigh of relief as we pull up outside. It is not what I expected the house to look like, but I am immensely glad that it is just perfectly normal.

Not worried about my Louboutins now I hop from the car and make my way towards the front door, Daniel comes running up behind me and stands by my side as I knock as pleasantly as I can. I could have let Daniel knock, but men knock loudly and it instantly puts you on guard as to who is on the other side. My knock could signify a cute little girl guide with cookies to sell or something along those gentle lines.

'Yes?' The lady that opens the door is tall and willowy with long dirty yellow hair and a lit cigarette hanging perilously from her bright red lips, the black and white ash getting ever longer.

She is a complete contrast to the rather curvaceous lady from last night. I can't very well ask if the woman with the shocking blue hair is home now can I.

'Hi, erm... is the homeowner available at all please?' It is the best I can do.

'If you're selling somet she won't be interested I can assure you.'

'Oh I'm not.' I smile, 'I met her last night and I completely forgot to ask her name, she has, well, blue hair?'

'Yeah, so what? What makes you think she'd wanna see

some random girl she met briefly in a club and narked off?' she growls at me.

'What's this?' Interrupts Daniel, 'Narked off how?' He looks at me puzzled.

'Came home she did banging on about your eyes, couldn't understand why you were so weird about it.'

'Well it's a sensitive issue for me to discuss with anyone, let alone complete strangers. Not that I have to explain myself to you.'

'And yet, here you are looking for said stranger. I can see why she'd have liked you.'

'Look, is she in or are you just wasting our time on purpose?'

'Oh she's in alright, but she's busy.'

'Please, it is really important that we speak with her.'

'She make you an offer or somet?' She asks cryptically.

'Sorry? An offer of what?' I ask impatiently.

She eyeballs me suspiciously, 'Oh never mind, always with the bloody secrets! I'll see if she's free.'

'Secrets?' Daniel asks her.

'Don't worry about it, Dendra is a mystery all of her own. I'll be back in a tick, stay there and don't go wondering about.'

'Why do you suppose she wants us to stay put?' Daniel asks me as she leaves, clearly puzzled.

'I don't know, how bizarre. I suppose we shall soon find out. Just wait until you meet Dendra.' I wink at him.

Distorted voices drift towards us from down the long narrow hallway that is visible from the door being left slightly ajar.

'Can you make out what they're saying?' Whispers Daniel, pressing his ear against the small opening.

I lean my head towards his and try to make out the hushed words.

'I don't know.' I shake my head, 'Sounds like the skinny one is saying *another done? another one?* Makes no sense.'

'Yeah probably unrelated anyway, we are way too suspicious.' laughs Daniel.

We are both chuckling at our eavesdropping when the door swings open and Dendra makes her grand appearance, I have a feeling that everything this woman does will be grand.

'Oh.' I gasp in shock, 'You have changed your hair.' Gone are the long blue locks of the previous evening, she is now sporting baby pink shoulder length curls, it surprisingly suits her.

'Wigs honey, no bad hair days ever again. Not that you've ever had a bad hair day I bet. Now, how can I help you? You didn't seem so eager to chat last night. I was surprised when Stella said that you were here.'

'We have a few questions for you Miss...?' Daniel intercepts.

'Brookes.' she smiles, 'but do please call me Dendra. Now just what kind of questions did you have in mind?'

'You were at L.U.V last night, Tiffany confirms that, but have you been to any of the other evenings since this place opened?'

'Yes actually. It's been open what... five weeks now. There's a dedicated singles night every Saturday, the rest of the week it's just a club with a luuurve theme.' She chuckles, 'I've been to every singles night since it opened. It's a nice vibe.'

'You see anything peculiar? Anything, oh let's say out of

the ordinary?'

'What exactly are you trying to ask me here? If you're talking about the missing girls then no, I saw nothing. But I wasn't exactly focusing my attention on anybody else now was I, had my own priorities if you know what I mean.'

'Did you ever leave with anybody that you met there?'

'If you're asking me if I've had one night stands then sure, who hasn't? Girl's gotta get her kicks any which way she can.'

'Oh my god seriously?' I screech, 'these guys could have all sorts of diseases, you should be more careful.'

'Oh, screen your dates do you princess? Full sexual health check before you drop your frilly knickers?'

'Of course not!' I fume, '*I* just have standards.'

'I'd be careful if I were you honey.' She jeers at Daniel, 'She'll have you down the clap clinic before you can even think second base.'

'How dare you! I will have you know that...'

'Ladies, ladies, please.' Groans Daniel, 'Can we just get this done?'

'Yes well. She started it.' I sniff.

'I think you'll find you started it when you insulted my personal life.' Dendra snaps back at me.

'Well I'm finishing it' sighs Daniel, 'If you don't mind my asking another question, did you ever stay over at the houses of the men you went with?'

'Sure, I mean I'm hardly gonna bring them back to my place now am I? That would be way too risky.'

'You ever see any dolls?' Daniel asks.

'Dolls? Honey these are grown men, why would they be playing with dolls?' She laughs. 'Nope never saw any dolls. Why? These guys into some freaky doll fetishes or what?'

'Doesn't matter.' Daniel shrugs noncommittally, 'just a thought.'

'Fair enough, well look I aint saying that they weren't into some kinky stuff, sure, you have to expect that from these kinds of places, but I never saw no dolls.'

'Why on earth would you sleep with these people?' I ask genuinely confused.

'Look sweetheart, it may be missionary all the way for you but I like a bit of spice in my life.'

'Spice?' I snort, 'is that what they call sexual diseases these days!'

'Okay, enough!' snaps Daniel again, 'This is getting us nowhere, it's like listening to squabbling sisters!'

'Whatever!' I gripe at them both. 'All I am saying is that I was evidently better educated in that department than some people.'

If I had to pinpoint the moment that Dendra's body language changed it would be the moment Daniel mentioned our being like sisters.

She had no come back to my continuing the argument, I felt for sure she would make some reference to my being better educated than she is, but nothing.

It is almost like a shadow has appeared, but only above her.

'Jeez, I'm sorry okay?' I mutter, 'No need to go all weird.'

'Have you ever had a sister?' she directs at me.

'No, had plenty of friends that I would have once classed as such though.'

'No, no that's not the same.' She is whispering, almost like she is in a trance. 'When you have a sister your whole world is perfect, she's the one friend that will always be there for you no matter what, she's the one you can always count on. And then... when she's gone...'

She trails off and I look at Daniel bemused.

'You had a sister?' asks Daniel gently.

'I guess I did.' She sighs. 'Now if you'll excuse me I have a million and one things to do, people to see and all of that.'

Like a switch being flicked she is back to her normal self. What the hell?

'Are you gonna be okay?' Daniel questions, 'you were a bit out of it a sec ago.'

'I'm good, thanks. You know, sometimes you just have to get on with things your own way.'

'Sure.' He agrees, 'well if you think of anything...' He hands her a business card *(where are my cards?)*

'Yeah, thanks.' She mutters, clearly going back into her trance. 'Well goodbye then.'

She closes the door firmly behind her as she enters the house, all is silent now.

'Can we go now? That was seriously messed up.' Daniel is eager to leave and we make our way to the car puzzled and unsure of what just happened.

'Do you think that she is hiding something?' I ask, 'I mean the way she suddenly went all zombiefied was not normal.'

'Yeah, something isn't sitting right with me; it could just be that she's recently bereaved and not dealing with it too well.'

'I suppose. We can check the Heaven records for that, so if she has recently lost a sister we could find out.'

'And if she hasn't?' he asks me.

'Then that woman is in need of a really good psychiatrist.'

'Let's check the records, if there is a record then we can try and get her some counselling, if there's nothing there then we can at least see if there's something else we can do to help her.'

'You seem awful keen to help.'

'Aaaw c'mon Tiff, you remember what it was like rocking up in Heaven all confused and upset. It's bad enough feeling that way and then being told that you are dead, but feeling that way and still having to get through every single day wishing you were dead must be terrible.'

'True. Okay let's see what we can do to help.' I smile. Daniels phone rings making us both jump in unison. How I wish he would change his ringtone, why on earth it has to always ring AC/DC Highway to Hell beats me, I mean he doesn't even like the Devil, and I would know.

His conversation is brief and throughout he looks amused, concerned and then finally sceptical.

Hanging up he turns to me, 'That was Fred, he's just had a man walk into the police station and say, *'I dreamt the kidnappings, I dreamt those poor girls.'*

The river becomes angry and swollen as the storm rages high above her; the clouds appear to have a sinister motive, rolling rapidly through the darkened sky to bring more rain, more devastation, their aim - to wreak havoc and destroy.

She stands frozen beside the river, she screams, her throat is raw, nobody can save her now.

Chapter Five

Fred is dead.

Oh we haven't just found him this way, he actually is dead. He's currently working undercover, trying to unearth corruption within his police department.

Fred helped me and Daniel on the first case that I was ever given – solving my own murder. *Nice!*

Anyway, we trust Fred implicitly and he in return regards us in the same manner, and gives us the heads up if he finds any leads.

The police themselves are of course working on this kidnapping case, but we are given these tasks to do to stop our brains turning to mush in Heaven. So we help out in the background where we can. If we catch the perpetrator then we let Fred know and he arrests them, and we get a nice pat on the back for all of our hard work *–not!*

'Guys he's a complete whacko, banging on about dreaming the kidnappings. I tell ya, every big crime we have has the nut jobs clambering out of their closets.'

'Know anything about him?' Daniel asks Fred.

'Yeah, ran a check. Single, no kids, no pets, no job, no previous. Guys as clean as they come, does however have over sixty two thousand friends on that Facebook thing.'

'Really?' I ask intrigued.

'Yeah, all following our chap in there. I had one of the reception girls check it out, no good with that computer wizardry malarkey me. Anyway Sheila said that the guy has dreams about all sorts of stuff, then he posts cryptic details about them on his wall and waits for people to

bite.'
'Bite?' Daniel asks, confused. 'I'm not following.'
'Yeah took me a while as well. He posts this stuff and waits for people to think it's about them.'
'Much like they do with horoscopes and the like.' I butt in. 'If you read horoscopes you can guarantee that something in there can be twisted by your very own brain to fit your current situation.'
'It's exactly like that. So he posts this stuff, waits for someone to think it's about them and charges them a handsome fee for full disclosure on the rest of the dream. I'd admire him for his ingenuity if he wasn't wasting police time.'
'People actually fall for this rubbish?' snorts Daniel.
'It would appear so. Names Leonard Critchin, he also goes by the name The Dreamcatcher.'

Sitting before Leonard I can't help but feel instantly sceptical. It isn't that I'm not a believer in such gifts; it's more that if a certain person were to be chosen to have such a power then why would it be this man Leonard Critchin?
I observed him whilst Daniel and Fred were talking, he has a strange tic. Nothing overly obvious, but if you watch for a while it is most definitely there.
Leonard Critchin blinks in a series of two's and three's. I wonder why he does such a thing and if it would be rude to enquire as to why?
'Mr Critchin.' Daniel extends his hand and makes our introductions, 'I have been informed that you may have some information for us on the recent kidnappings?'
Leonard Critchin takes Daniel's hand and shakes it

vigorously, never losing eye contact and never dropping the smile that he has fixed in place.

'I wasn't sure whether or not to bother the police with my information, people can be so sceptical about my work, you have no idea how exhausting it is to constantly be mocked.'

'But surely Mr Critchin...' I begin, '...you are not mocked so much that it has damaged your reputation to foretell people of their futures. You are still managing well financially I should imagine.'

'It isn't all about the monetary aspect you understand Miss Delamarre, the things I see are not always for the better. Trust me when I say that passing on damaging news is not a pleasure for me.' He sighs and continues, 'Sometimes I have to tell a follower that he or she may have a family member that is sick or going to die, sometimes it is the follower themselves. It is not a joy to pass on such tragic news, and there you see Miss Delamarre is when my gift becomes a curse.'

'I imagine that you still charge for this *'news'* though?'

'We all have a living to make, please do not judge me on mine. I was given this gift, this curse, whatever you may call it, and it is my duty to ensure that whatever channels through me is passed on accordingly. I did not ask for this life.'

'How do these dreams come about then?' asks Daniel, 'Are they like normal dreams, the kind of dreams that I would have myself for example?'

Leonard leans towards Daniel and takes his hand, 'If only it were so simple. Hear me when I say that if you ever had a dream that felt so real, that made you believe that everything that you were thinking and feeling was genuine and happening right there and then, then know this, those are mere droplets of what I experience, for I am there, right in the middle of whatever nightmare chooses to invade my unconscious state. I cannot move, I cannot scream, I am alone in a nightmare that seems never to end.'

Silence stretches its bony fingers all around the interview room, and I shudder at how pained and hollow Leonard looks.

'Are these not simply night terrors Mr Critchin? I have done my fair share of reading over the years and these sound exactly like night terrors.'

'Night terrors would be a walk in the park compared to these horrors. It is like I am there right at that very moment. If one of my followers is to be killed in a stabbing, it is me that is stabbed first. I feel every inch of the knife entering my body, I feel the blood oozing from me as I fight to take my last breath, I feel death quickly approaching me and I feel the moment that my body closes down forever. These are no night terrors Daniel, this is real.'

'And you charge to pass on this information?' I ask, 'you let a person know that they are going to be stabbed to death and then ask how they plan to pay?'

'You make it sound so cold.' He whispers.

'Well it kind of is.' I answer icily.

'Can you tell us about the dream that you had of the missing girls now Leonard?' Interrupts Daniel, glaring at me.

Leonard closes his eyes as the room falls silent once more.

'I saw colours, lots of different colours. Orange, red, blue, pink. Always different colours.

I heard screaming, then muffled murmurs as though a gag had been used.

I smelt something that made me wrinkle my nose, like the smells in a hospital, from those dispensers that you put antibacterial gel on from.

A voice said 'set up the monitor and the speakers.'

I saw the girl, the last one that was taken. Her blonde hair was all matted from the struggle.

A hand was trying to free the knots and tangles; I could not tell if the hand belonged to a woman or a man. The girl screamed in pain from the brushing of her hair. The hand slowed, careful not to hurt her again.

The girl is left in the dark, a small room.

I heard static from a TV, like a humming sound.

Then voices, played over and over and over again. The same words. I cannot hear what they are.

The girl screams, she does not stop screaming.

Air vent opens slightly, powder, the woman sleeps.'

We wait patiently for Leonard to open his eyes. He looks dazed, slightly confused.

'Would you like some water?' I ask him quietly.

He shakes his head, 'No, no thank you.'

Standing he wobbles slightly and Daniel reaches to take his arm.

'Okay, steady there.' Daniel laughs, 'Let's get you some fresh air okay.'

Leonard nods and as he is escorted from the interview room I notice that there are words scratched into the desk. YES. YES. NO.

Darting from the room I ask Leonard about the words. He smiles weakly at me and says 'I was answering my calls.'

'He's confused Tiff, we can find out later okay.'

'No, it's not okay. I want to know now. Leonard, what do you mean?'

He takes my hands in his, 'Sometimes my dreams come to me whilst I'm awake, a little like day dreaming. I know that you noticed me blinking, well that's my way of answering them. But, I was busy with you and Daniel here with my eyes closed, so I had to answer some other way.'

'Do you normally vandalise property answering these calls?' I ask.

'Of course not, I normally have a pen and paper to hand.'

'C'mon Leonard, let's get you home.' Sighs Daniel, 'get you back to your missed calls.'

'You may be sceptical of my gift Mr Fox, but mocking a man for being something unique is rich coming from somebody in your position.'

Daniel coughs, 'and what position would that be?'

'Why, being the walking dead of course.'

Chapter Six

The lack of any real clues from Leonard Critchin has me heading in search of Celestia, maybe a fresh pair of ears on the subject will help somehow. Daniel and I hashed it out as best we could, but in the end we were more confused than when we started.

Voices, powder, colours, television, antibacterial gel? How are we supposed to decipher that?

Not to mention how on earth did he know that we are no longer mortal?

Do we give off some deceased like aroma?

Are we so obviously dead?

I looked at myself in the mirror for a long time after his statement and I have to say that I look just as fabulous as ever!

Whatever his reasons for declaring our current state of lifelessness, he did not seem in the slightest bit concerned or frightened.

Maybe he does have a gift.

Celestia's office is in complete darkness as I ease open the door.

'Celestia.' I call out, 'Are you in here?'

A muffled voice echoes out from behind the desk and as I crouch down to take a look I find her, curled up in a little ball sobbing. Reaching out I touch her arm, 'What is wrong?' I ask her quietly, 'Celestia?'

'Go away Tiffany.' She hiccups, 'Just go away.'

'I can't very well go away now can I? Not when you are here, in the dark crying like this.'

'Well I never asked you to come in here did I!' She snaps at me.

Taking a deep breath, I rein my annoyance back in and ask her again what is wrong. 'You may as well tell me, because I have no intentions of leaving you here like this.'

'Oh why do you have to be here Tiffany? Why you?'

'I've asked myself that question a million times, believe me.' I laugh, 'Still have no answer though, so I guess you are stuck with me.'

'It's all too much you know, all of this.' She waves her arm carelessly around her.

'The job?' I ask her. 'Maybe you could get an assistant?'

'No silly girl.' She snaps, 'Not the job! Everything!'

'Mmm you know this really doesn't seem to be making too much sense. Why don't you start at the beginning and we will see if we can figure this mess out?'

'Oh! And what makes you think you can help me?'

'Nothing to be perfectly honest, but I don't see anybody else in this room offering, do you?'

Shuffling from under the desk she flops down into her chair and puts her head in her hands. 'It's no use; no matter what I do I just can't find a way out of this mess. Oh what have I done?' She cries and I debate whether or not to put a comforting arm around her, I choose not, she will no doubt berate me for doing so.

'What has happened?'

'He's dead, oh Tiffany he has died and I have not helped. What kind of a person does that make me?'

'Who has died?'

'Godfrey. My husband.'

Is it just me or is it weird that Celestia and Godfrey have some seriously weird Heaven related names going on?

'Right. And why does Godfrey dying make you a bad person? People die all of the time.'

'Because.' She sobs, 'Because I've left him.'

'You left him a long time ago Celestia, I'm sure he's dealt with it. Didn't you say he had remarried?' A thought suddenly hits me, 'Oh god, his new wife isn't here as well is she?'

'No'

'So what actually is the issue here then?'

'Godfrey is dead and I haven't even been to see him.'

'Well it's not like he knows you are here running the place is it?'

'Oh it's worse than that. He's dead, he's here and I have had him locked away in interview room two for the past four days.'

'Erm... why?'

'Because I can't face him!' She screams and I take a step back, Celestia is losing the plot right in front of my eyes. 'I can't see him, what if I still have feelings for him, how can I see him?'

'Because it's your job.' I tell her sternly, 'because no matter your feelings you still have a position to uphold here. Now, wipe your eyes and let's go and get Godfrey out of that horrible room!'

'But what if...'

'But what if nothing! Feelings or no feelings you can't keep him locked away in there.' I take her hand and smile encouragingly, 'I will be with you, and we can deal with the emotional side of this dilemma once we have set him free, okay?'

'What if it's not okay?' she cries.

'I can't answer that, all you can do is see him and see what happens. You remember when you arrived here don't you?'

'Yes, very well as a matter of fact.' She sniffs.

'And do you think that was made easier or harder by having someone there to help you and guide you?'

'Easier of course.'

'Right then, so what is stopping you right now from making this transition easier for Godfrey?'

'Because...' she hiccups, 'because I still love him.'

'Then be there for him.'

Shoving Celestia into interview room two I sit and wait out the inevitable.

There will no doubt be shouting, denial of the situation, crying and finally acceptance.

I guess that I can understand where Celestia was coming from when she panicked and hid her ex husband away, not wanting the face the truth. After all how will I feel when I am confronted with people that I know arriving here?

My parents especially.

It would not be so bad if my parents were normal. You know, the kind that don't use your wake as a chance to expand their social circle, the kind that don't clear away your belongings before you are cold in your grave and remove all photographs of your beautiful smiling face.

Nice!

I hope that I do not see them again anytime soon.

Two hours later my legs are going numb from all of this sitting around.

Daniel popped by and we had another chat about the clues that the Dreamcatcher left us. We are still none the wiser as to what he was droning on about.

How does he even get paid for this?

I fill Daniel in on what I'm doing loitering in the corridor, but I leave out the bit about Celestia stashing her husband away like some dirty secret, I have a feeling that she would not want anybody else to know that.

I promise to catch up with Daniel later in the restaurant *(he's always eating)* and stand to stretch my legs for what feels like the ten millionth time.

Finally the door creaks open and Celestia pops her tear stained face around it to peer at me.

'We are going to be a while longer.' She sniffs. 'It's okay, I don't need you to hang around anymore now.'

'Is everything okay?' I ask her concerned.

'Yes, yes of course, you were right, I should have dealt with this situation a lot better.' She smiles.

'Of course I was right.' I grin, 'I am Tiffany Delamarre.'

◇

There is only silence as she begs and pleads for her to breathe. To take just one breath that will hopefully lead onto more.

But she does not. Not breathing! Not breathing!

Her lips are blue, her pink nightdress torn and sodden, how can this be she wonders, she was fine before, just fine.

Wind howls around her, laughing at her torture, taunting her for her very own cruelty.

She deserves this, she deserves this punishment and torment, but the girl beneath her does not.

She begs for God to trade places, to let it be her laying there in the mud, but he does not listen.

Pressing her lips against the girl's she breathes deeply into her mouth, her tears running down onto her cheeks, her prayers remaining unanswered still.

In the movies she thinks a tear and a whispered I love you would fix everything, but this is not a movie and it would seem there will be no happy ending. Why did she tease her?

Why did she have to be relentless in her mockery? Why won't she breathe?

Chapter Seven

'Tell me again why we are doing this?' I grumble.
Daniel and I are currently elbow deep in slimy mud and god knows what else slowly approaching the residence of Dendra Brookes.
It is way past midnight; I am tired, filthy and not impressed in the slightest.
'Because records had nothing on Dendra having lost a sister.' He whispers.
'Well maybe she's just some crazy fantasist that enjoys sympathy for made up losses.' I suggest.
'No, it's more than that. They had a partial record of another family member, a female that was close to deaths door, but it never came about. So dear Tiffany, where is that family member now?'
'You think she has her hidden away?' I laugh, 'And I thought my ideas were farfetched.'
'You're ideas normally are.'
'So here we are, in the middle of the night, staking out her house in the hope of finding some random family member who may or may not be important to our case?'
'Yep. Pretty much.'
'But why would she be part of our case Daniel? So the woman has a sick relative, that doesn't mean that she knows anything about the kidnappings?'
'Maybe not, but it would explain the antibacterial gel that Leonard could smell in his dreams. Sick people = Antibacterial gel = No germs.'
'Plenty of people use antibacterial gel, myself included.'

'Can we just check it out? If nothing comes of it we can find a new lead. This is the only thing that we have Tiff, and right now any direction is better than no direction.'

The house is in complete darkness apart from one tiny orange light coming from what looks like a basement. Considering my past experiences with basements I am not too keen to go in there, but Daniel insists and I would rather be with him in the basement than left out here in the middle of a field all by myself.
Making our way through the mud and wet grass we kneel beneath the basement window and try to peek inside.
'Can you see anything?' I stage whisper.
'No. Not a thing. C'mon let's have a look around.'
Tiptoeing past the basement and the kitchen, we find ourselves in a large yard.
In the far left hand corner is a concrete shed, and to the right two large Biffa bins. The rest of the yard is empty and swept clean of any debris.
'Now what?' I ask frustrated, 'a shed and two bins, hardly the crime of the century.'
'But what's in the shed and the bins?' He grins at me.
'I am absolutely not rummaging through a bin, not a chance.'
Laughing Daniel pulls me towards the shed, 'Okay, you do the shed, I'll do the bins.'

The shed is locked, but I soon manage to prise open the flimsy lock. Tracey and her previous life of stealing have really come in handy tonight. She thought it would be fun a little while back to show me how to pick a lock and open a door with a credit card, I am glad that I paid attention now.

Inside the shed everything is covered in plastic sheeting. It is spotlessly clean, no dust, no spider webs, no creepy crawlies.

Pulling my gloves further up my wrists I begin to peel back the plastic to reveal the contents underneath.

I am confronted with two mattresses and a really old looking wheelchair. The mattresses look brand new. Pulling them forward I look behind them and see nothing but emptiness. So, basically a whole shed for two mattresses and an old wheelchair.

There is nothing else of particular interest in the shed, and maybe the wheelchair was used for this elusive family member and they are better now. Either way this feels like a complete waste of my time.

Pulling the plastic carefully back into position I put the lock back on and creep across the yard to find Daniel.

'Have you found anything oh handsome bin dweller?'

Puffing and panting his head appears over the top of the bin, 'sure have.' Jumping out from the bin as noiselessly as he can he thrusts a tube into my hands whilst he reaches back into grab something else. 'See? Proof that someone here is hiding something.'

'So what. What is this junk anyway?'

'It's a feeding tube, and this...' he wiggles a smaller plastic tube in front of my face, '...is a catheter.'

Dropping the tube with a screech I step backwards and crash into the bin behind me, the lid slams down with a loud clang and I watch in horror as a light from an upstairs room in the house flickers on.

'Erm Tiff, back up quietly and then run!'

Grabbing my hand we run across the field as fast as we

can go, my lungs feel fit to burst but Daniel drags me until we are clear of the house.

'I'm so sorry.' I pant, exhausted, 'that was close.'

'C'mon let's get out of here.'

Heaven is a hive of activity when we return and we soon find out from the hoard of screaming girls that some hunky pop star has recently perished and they are all eager to have a look at him. *Idiots!*

Celestia is manning the corridor with Godfrey at her side. I wonder how this is going to work out now. Do they just pick up where they left off? What happens when the other wife eventually arrives here? I sure hope that she knows what she's doing.

'...you threw a catheter at me!' I yell in response to Daniel telling me off for making so much noise. '... A bloody catheter! What did you want me to do? Smile and be thankful?'

'I did not throw it at you, I merely showed you what I had found.'

'Whatever! Either way what does a catheter and a feeding tube prove? That Dendra has a sick relative? Wow, case closed!'

Daniel takes a deep breath, 'no, it proves that she needs help if nothing else. But... I asked if she had a sister and she said that she guesses she did.'

'So maybe she's really sick Daniel, it doesn't mean that she has any involvement whatsoever in this case.'

'What is it with you Tiff? At any other time you'd have been all over this theory like a rash, and now... this?'

'Please do not ever refer to me again in the same sentence

as the word rash!'

'Well what is it then?'

I sigh, 'you heard Celestia, saying that I always have some ridiculous theory, well maybe I just want to prove her wrong on something.'

'Well let's prove her wrong on this. Anyway this isn't your theory, the doll connection is yours.'

'Oh sure, now we have an ill relative and dolls to throw into the mix. If Dendra had a sister then I think she would be a little past playing with dolls by now. Maybe the whole doll idea was a little bit too much of a leap, maybe dolls have nothing to do with this at all.'

'Or, maybe Dendra is living in the past, maybe these women look like her sister, relative, whatever and she's trying to keep a hold on the past.'

'Surely then she would kidnap children not full grown adults.'

'Okay.' He begins to pace, 'Maybe these women resemble the relative in some way? What if they were being kidnapped so that Dendra could pretend they were her sister, not sick, not dying, just there.'

'For what purpose? That's the thought process of a mad person, and despite Dendra being a tad loose on her sexual morals she didn't strike me as being mad.'

'Can we at least pay her a visit and ask again about the sister? If nothing else we can get her some help.'

'Fine. But I think this all some crazy wild goose chase.'

'There's something here Tiff, I can feel it.'

'I hope so, because it's been nearly a week now. Another woman is surely due to be taken.'

Chapter Eight

Paying Leonard Critchin a visit is my idea.

Daniel believes the man a lot more than I do, but, there were medical supplies at Dendra's house, which in turn would lead to the use of antibacterial gel, and I just feel that maybe he might be of some use again. I'm not saying that his gifts are real, that his dreams can predict the future, but there is some small part of me that wants to believe.

I would never in a million years have dreamt that when I died I would experience the things that I have, that I would fall in love with an angel and spend my days solving crimes, but here I am doing just that.

So maybe Leonard Critchin isn't all deception and financial gain, maybe just maybe there is some truth behind what he sees.

Daniel hands Leonard the feeding tube, we felt the catheter was totally inappropriate.

'Can you get readings off of objects?' he asks.

'In some instances yes, but generally it is just when said object is personal to an individual.'

'I don't think you can get much more personal than something that was thrust down their throat Leonard.'

'Yes, well. Let us see what we can get shall we.'

He leads us through to a small room at the rear of the property, pointing for us to take a seat in the corner while he sets up.

This is a nice room, oddly peaceful and slightly mystical. Crystals hang from the windows and as the sunlight catches them it makes little rainbows appear against the walls. I like it here.

Leonard takes the feeding tube and places it against his face as he lies on the single bed that is pushed into the corner opposite the sofa's.

I try not to gag at the thought of where that tube has been. As Leonard closes his eyes his hands grip tighter around the tube, his face distorts and his breathing becomes laboured.

'Erm, Daniel? Should we get some help?'

Daniel shushes me, 'I think it's just part of the process honey, just leave him to get on with it.'

A scream echoes around the room, Leonard is convulsing, thrashing from side to side as his hands grip the tube so hard that it bends beneath his fingers.

As quickly as the scream begins it ends, the room falls into deathly silence as Leonard's voice whispers into the room.

'There is a river, in the darkness. The rain beats down; she runs but cannot see where she is going. She is being chased, she cannot be caught, it will all start again if she is caught. The chaser is gaining ground, the wind picks up speed now throwing her off balance. She falls.

A bed, beeping, warmth, but no comfort. She does not like it in this room with these people.

Crying all around her.

A room, it smells of hospitals again but it is a different room. She cannot move.

Beep. Beep. Beep.

A tube. This tube.

She cannot breathe, she panics, but she cannot move away from the hurt.

She wants to be left alone; she wants to be away from this

person that she ran from. But still they torment her.
Hell. Hell. Hell.
She sleeps, but it is not restful.
She dreams. Nightmares. Reruns. She will never be free.'

Leonard awakens with a start and I am surprised to find that I have been crying.
Who is this poor girl?
'If you will just excuse me for one moment while I freshen up.' Leonard leaves the room, he looks pale and shaken.
'Do you believe now?' Asks Daniel.
'Who is this girl Daniel?'
'I don't know honey but we need to find out and fast.'
'I guess that Dendra doesn't have anything to do with the kidnappings, but she sure as hell has something to do with the torture of this girl.'
'She sure does. We need to get in there Tiff.'
I think for a moment. 'Leonard said Hell three times.'
'Yeah?'
'Do you think he meant actual Hell?'
'Tiff we are not speaking to the Devil, no way, no how. The guy is a maniac!'
'It was just a thought.'
'Promise me...'
'I won't seek out Lucifer I promise.'
'Tiff I mean it. That guy has got it bad for you, he'd stop at nothing to get you down there.'
'Well then that's his problem, the heat would play havoc with my hair anyway.' I laugh.
'Tiff!'
'Okay, okay.'
'Sorry about that.' Smiles Leonard, 'I hope that you got

what you needed?'

'We did and some.' Replies Daniel sadly, 'I just wish it weren't the case.'

'Not all dreams should be disclosed, some should be left hidden, buried far away.'

'Do you keep some hidden?' I ask.

'I know that you think I am only in this for the money Miss Delamarre, but I take my gift seriously. If I dream a dream so horrific that the person knowing it would be driven insane with worry then I will never disclose.'

'But you do disclose some dreams where an individual is to be killed – you told us that at the police station. Would that not drive a person insane with worry? Wondering when it will happen?'

'Of course. But I disclose those snippets as a sign, the future can be altered Miss Delamarre, and if you knew that you were going to die in some random attack that was not personally aimed at you, just wrong place, wrong time, would you not want to know? Would you not like to be given the chance to change it?'

'Of course I would. But I would still spend my days and nights worrying about when it was coming.'

'So you would rather not know? What if I could tell you that you were to die outside of a jewellers, a robbery gone wrong – would that not ensure that you would steer clear of the jewellers?'

'Yes, I suppose it would.' I admit reluctantly. 'But what kind of dreams would you keep away from a person if not those?'

'The kind where I cannot give them any clues as to where or when their death, or the death of a loved one would take place. How could I share that a person is to die tragically and not tell them how, where or when? Nobody could live knowing that. Knowing that something horrific was to happen, but they were clueless as to when. That would surely drive you insane.'

'What about that dream? Would you have let somebody claim that one?'

'Yes. Because somebody somewhere needs help, and they need it fast.'

Damien looks surprised to see us as we stand smiling on his doorstep holding a bottle of whiskey and a catheter.

The catheter was Daniel's idea of a joke.

'Such wonderful gifts you bring me.' He retorts drily. 'How have I ever managed without such generous friends.'

'Friends? You?' I laugh, '*Hardly*.'

'Ah Tiffany, a pleasure as always.'

'The pleasure is most definitely yours.'

'How long has it been now since I last saw you? And still with the bad attitude.'

'Clearly not long enough. And just because I dislike these places does not mean that I have a bad attitude.'

'Regardless, it is good to see you both. Now, what can I do for you?' He directs the question at Daniel, dismissing me, as usual.

'We need your help with something, and it's a little unorthodox.' Explains Daniel, 'Are we okay to come in for a moment?'

'Please do. And I would be surprised if you ever needed help of a different nature.'

Daniel explains to Damien the case so far, the Dreamcatcher and also the dream. He sits engrossed as the story unfolds.

'And where do I come into all of this?' He asks puzzled. 'Surely if this girl is still alive then it is not my particular services that you require at present.'

'We need a distraction, something to get us into that house.'

'Right. And you think an Embalmer will give you such a way in?'

'A funeral Director would be a perfect distraction, even if we can't get in, we may overhear enough to know that there is somebody in there that needs help.'

'I see. This is incredibly unprofessional you understand?'

'Please Damien, you know that we wouldn't ask if it wasn't important. You also know that I wouldn't step foot in this place in my Louboutins if we weren't desperate.'

'What a natural way you have of being rude and yet asking for assistance in the sweetest of manners.'

'Will you help us or not?' I demand.

'And there she is... the genuine Tiffany Delamarre.'

Sulking I ask him politely if he will help us.

'Of course, I never had any intention of saying no.'

'You are such a drain on my life.' I groan.

'Quite.' He grins.

'The plan is simple, you rock up to the house, do your usual chatter and we try and get in through the back. If she tries to usher you away, then remain insistent that you are here to do... well, whatever it is you do.'

'Leave it with me. I can sense a dying person from a mile away.'

'What a delightful skill.' I snort.

'Well, I knew what you were the moment I clapped eyes on you.'

'No you did not! I don't even look dead.'

'To the untrained eye maybe not, but you my dear are as dead as they come.'

Chapter Nine

We wait until nightfall before we send Damien in. Our thoughts are that if Dendra is disorientated from being awoken so abruptly then she may inadvertently open up.
We watch as Damien makes his way towards the front door and knocks as loudly as he can.
After a few tense moments a light flickers on upstairs and we take this as our signal to get ourselves into position.
We are now crouched down to the left of Damien with the plan that once he engages her in conversation we will make our way to the basement and go in through the window there. Daniel said that when we were here last it looked loose and should open with not too much effort or noise involved.
A light flickers into life as Damien knocks forcefully upon Dendra's door. I do not know how well this is going to go down, but we need to gain access to that house and sharpish.
Daniel and I have crept around to the side of the building and are currently knelt, *yes knelt*, behind a large foul smelling Biffa bin and I am not in the slightest bit impressed.
I pray, I really do that one day I may be lucky enough to have a case that is clean, easy, sophisticated and above all does not involve my beautiful new Hunter wellington boots being caked in mud.
'When Damien goes inside make your way to the window okay, I'll go in first and help you down.' Whispers Daniel all action man like.

Daniel has already removed the board that was covering the small window to the basement - *thank god I didn't have that extra pancake for breakfast this morning* - now all we need is a distraction to get inside.

'Can I help you?' Yawns a bedraggled looking Dendra. Wow, she could have at least run a brush through her wiry orange mop before answering the door.

'My apologies for your loss Miss Brookes, I appreciate that this is a difficult time.' Damien's voice is sombre and ever so slightly grim reaper-ish. 'If you would be kind enough to show me to...'

'What?' snaps Dendra, 'what the hell are you talking about difficult time? What difficult time? Who are you?'

'My name is Damien Kernick, from Kernick Family Funeral Home, I received a telephone call informing me that...'

'Funeral home?!' she screeches, 'Is this some sick joke?'

'I assure you Miss Brookes that I do not see the passing of a loved one at all amusing.'

'Passing! Are you completely deranged? Let me see some I.D, now!'

'Go.' whispers Daniel in my ear, 'it's now or never.'

Pushing myself forward through the mud, I am about to peek my head around the side of the bin when torch light illuminates it, ducking back quickly I cross my fingers and hope that I was not spotted.

'Wha...'

'Shush.' Turning to Daniel I point to the light and shrug my shoulders, 'now what?'

Old dead leaves crunch underfoot as the unknown makes their way towards us, if we are caught now then it's game over, all of this set up will have been for nothing.

Silence falls over the yard, other than Dendra's heavy outraged breathing and a rustling noise which I assume is Damien retrieving his identification there is not a sound to be heard.

'Why those bloody kids! I swear to god if I get my hands on those little scratters I will ring their bloody necks!' We watch in horror as Dendra's housemate Stella begins to replace the boarding that Daniel not so long ago removed. 'Great, just bloody great! They've stolen the nails! Dendra you have just got to see this!'

'Not now!' screeches Dendra snatching Damien's driving licence, 'I have a bigger problem here than those bleedin' kids!'

'Eh? You said it was just someone coming to the wrong address and to go back to bed - well good job I got up isn't it.'

'Just go inside Stella I can deal with this.'

'I will, right after I've fixed the boarding on the basement window - then I suggest you have a strong drink and think about an apology for your tone.'

'Oh just get inside will you!'

As Stella stomps back into the house to find more nails Daniel nudges me forward.

'We can still get in there if we are quick.' He urges. 'There is no chance that we will make it now, not to mention how do we get back out again if she nails the window back shut? We'll just have to find another way.'

Shuffling further back behind the bin I draw my legs up underneath my chin and pull my coat tighter around me, it's freezing sitting here on the mud and all I want to do is go home now. It's been a wasted night, we have discovered nothing at all of any use and poor Damien has potentially dented his reputation on a fruitless venture.

'You need to leave before I call the police.' yells Dendra, 'in fact, I think I will call them anyway.'

'If the police are contacted Miss Brookes then they too will wish to gain access to your property, and I can understand why you do not want your sister to be taken away, but that is the inevitable conclusion to this sad situation.'

'I do not have a dead sister!' she screeches, 'who called you?' she demands fiercely.

'I am afraid that I am not at liberty to divulge that information.' He sighs, 'Miss Brookes, the hour is late and all I wish to do is my job, with as little emotional distress for you as I can, may I therefore suggest that you take a moment with your sister and then let me take care of the rest.'

'My sister is not dead! How many more times do I have to tell you?!'

The air crackles with newly shed developments and I can feel the hairs on the back of my neck and my arms rising in anticipation.

Her sister is not dead.

As Damien glances briefly our way and Daniel nods his agreement to now leave, Damien makes his apologies and promises to look into the matter further, and ensures Dendra that she will not be bothered by his company again in relation to this unfortunate misunderstanding.

'Yeah, you do that! And don't you dare come here again!'

Slamming the door into Damien's bemused face I can't help but snigger at the slip up.

'Who goes there?' demands the croaky voice of Stella. In our excitement we had completely forgotten that Stella was re-attaching the broken board.

'Well?' she demands.

'Run.' whispers Daniel, 'now!'

Squelching in the mud I slip and slide until Daniel pulls me upright, then we are running as fast as our mud laden boots will allow towards Damien's van.

'Stop right there!' Stella yells. 'I'm warning you!'

I can't help the giggle that escapes my lips as I imagine her chasing us with her broken bit of board and a few rusty nails.

Damien screeches away as we fasten our seatbelts, laughing at the sight of Stella in the mirrors shaking her fist in the air and turning it blue with her foul language.

Back at Damien's place we are huddled around the grand fireplace in the main lounge watching the flames dance happily, lost in our own thoughts of what to do with the information that we now have.

'I guess she just needs help then.' Sighs Daniel.

'Rather that than her be our kidnapper.' I smile, 'I know it's disappointing but we will just have to keep looking for our lady snatcher, and as lucky as it would have been to just stumble upon them like that I feel kind of relieved that it's not Dendra.'

'I know what you're saying honey, I just had a feeling ya know?'

'Tea is served.' Booms Damien, 'C'mon chin up, at least something good came out of tonight.'

'Oh and what's that?' mumbles Daniel forlornly.

'Well other than seeing our delightful Tiffany here up to her eyeballs in mud...' he laughs, '...You do at least know that dear Dendra needs help and now you can make sure that she gets it.'

'Ha! Hilarious grim reaper boy, you're splitting my sides!' I sneer in his direction.

'Now, now guys - no fighting. It's been a long night already and I can't handle you two bickering.'

'So what are you going to do about getting her some help?' Damien continues, still obviously amused judging by the smirk on his face.

'She definitely said that her sister isn't dead, but what confuses me is that Heaven had a partial record from a long time ago of a relative who was potentially heading their way, but that never happened, so if it was her sister then where on earth has she been hiding, because Dendra would only have been a child herself.' I muse aloud.

'Maybe she was in some kind of care home until Dendra was old enough to care for her?' Replies Damien, all traces of his earlier sarcasm gone.

'Then why the secrecy?' Asks Daniel, 'It just doesn't make an ounce of sense.'

'I think we should pay another visit to Dendra, try and get her to open up to us. Maybe tonight's escapades will make her realise that there is help out there if she just asks.' I declare happily, 'We can help her Daniel, all we have to do is make her see that we are not the enemy.'

'Yeah, and in the meantime we still have a kidnapper to find.'

'Other than that freak with the trains we have nothing.'

'You mean Albert?' I ask.

'I mean what I say... the freak with the trains.'

'Okay okay he's a creepy freak, but I'm not convinced, why would he - collector of trains suddenly become a collector of blondes?'

'Because he's a freak Tiff.'

'Fair enough.' I laugh tiredly. 'Can we go home now?'

'Yep. Thanks for tonight Damien, really appreciate it.'

'Not a problem.' Yawns Damien, 'You'd think I would be used to these unsociable hours.' He laughs. 'You know the saying... I'll get enough sleep when I'm dead? Really doesn't mean anything to you two does it judging by how exhausted you look.'

'Nah, even the dead have to sleep eventually.' winks Daniel.

'Yes, no rest for the wicked... as they say.' I smile cheekily, 'No rest for them at all.'

Chapter Ten

'Shush, don't let her hear you.'

Making my way over to where Victoria and Tracey are grinning like utter loons in the restaurant I slide into a seat and grin right back.

The place is full to bursting with hungry deceased folk and I can only assume that there has been a sudden influx of people from the queue. Happens that way sometimes, quiet one minute and crazy mad the next. Must be the season for high mortality rates. *Poor schmucks.*

I am surprised to find Daniel missing in action, on any other day where there is food there is Daniel Fox, plate in hand and asking for thirds.

'Wow - could you make it any more obvious that you are talking about me girls, I mean honestly.' I laugh.

'Ah we were just having you on.' smirks Tracey, 'we knew you were there.'

'So how are things?' I ask, 'It seems like a total age since I saw you both last, any goss?'

'Things are better.' shrugs Victoria.

'Better than what?' I ask confused, 'Have I missed something? What has happened?'

'The Devil wanted to send Jeffrey up here, apparently he doesn't feel that he's a good fit in Hell and it isn't the place for him.' Victoria sighs.

Spluttering my Earl Grey in a most unlady like fashion I gawk at Victoria and then at Tracey, 'You are kidding me?'

'Nope. So it would seem that when good old Lucifer tires

of his little evil minions, or feels that they are not worthy of being in his kingdom he tries to palm them off to Heaven. Luckily Celestia and the judges put a stop to it.'

'How can he just do that? I mean, they are down there for a reason, he can't just decide to send them here. What about the victims of those people, how are they supposed to feel about that?' I ask angrily, that man sure has a lot to answer for.

'Celestia said that his requests for transfers are always denied.' shrugs Tracey, 'doesn't stop him from trying though.''

'Well I can absolutely guarantee he will not be trying again after I have finished with him.'

'Oh no, no way Tiff, look at what happened last time you decided to take a little jaunt to Hell. Celestia was not best pleased and you and Tracey had to face the judges. It's not worth it. He always gets refused anyway, so why put yourself in that horrible situation again.'

Sighing as I know that Victoria is right, I go to refill my now cold tea and ponder on why the Devil is such a moron.

I get that he is bad, of course I do. That is why he has his own kingdom of debauchery, but surely somewhere inside of him he must know and understand that his actions are completely misguided and quite frankly immoral.

What if he ever decided that Juliana was no longer of any use to him? Would he try and get rid of her also? Over my dead and seriously fabulous body is that ever going to happen.

Sitting back down with the girls I feel a sense of home, of belonging. I would never have entertained either of them when I was alive, in fact I barely tolerated them when I died. But they have become such great friends to me; I know that they will always look out for me, just as I know that I will always look out for them.

I do not deserve them, truly I do not. Not after the way that I treated them, but unlike me they are selfless and forgiving and kind, something I strive daily to become.

'Is everything okay with you Tracey?' I ask with a smile.

'All good chick... it's all good.' she laughs confidently.

Tracey had a difficult life, a constant barrage of abuse and unpleasantness. She was desperately unhappy and eager to leave the world as she knew it far behind.

Tracey grew up with an alcoholic Father after the death of her Mother when she was just a baby; poor girl never stood a chance.

Her Father beat her on a regular basis, spent all of their money on booze and cigarettes and eventually it just ground her down.

She had thought about taking her own life, and in the end the decision was made for her as she was hit by a bus. Her own Father never even attended her funeral. Probably too wasted to notice she was gone.

'And you Tiff? How are you?'

'We have another case.' I sigh. 'Lots of dead ends, no real clues and no matter what we do we just can't seem to get in front.'

'Well if I know you...' winks Tracey, 'You will have the culprit caught in no time.'

If only I could believe that, I think to myself, if only...

'Tiff?' Shouts Daniel from the restaurant door, 'let's go.'

'Just who are you bossing around Fox?' I shout back. There is silence as he walks towards me, determined yet uneasy. My stomach plummets as I recognise the look of dread on his face. 'We have another missing woman.'

Jumping from my seat I rush from the restaurant with Daniel hot on my heels.

How are we going to stop this maniac?

Chapter Eleven

'Name's Marcy Grey, it's been confirmed this morning by her flatmate Jenny Lewis that she attended the singles night two nights ago.' Fred our undercover dead copper flips his notebook shut and looks around the now deserted nightclub. 'Reported missing this morning.'

'How come it took her flatmate so long to report her gone?' I ask.

If one of my girls hadn't made contact with me for even a few hours I would have totally flipped out, never mind two days. Would they have done the same for me though?

Doubtful with what I now know.

'Jenny made it clear that she's a bit of a party animal, not one to shy away from the odd one night stand. Said she figured she'd stretched the one night over an extra day. Started panicking when she didn't answer her calls or text messages.'

'And Jenny is definitely sure that she made it here?'

'Yep. Said she dropped her right at the front door and watched her go in. Her attendance has also been confirmed by the event organiser Lizzie Carver. Mobile goes straight to voicemail, no social media updates, nothing.'

'Some friend.' I mutter under my breath.

'Can the phone not be tracked?'

'It's off. So either it's out of charge or whoever has her has turned it off.'

'What does she look like?' questions Daniel.

'Same as the rest.' Fred replies despondently, 'Long blonde hair, petite, pretty...'

'You got a list of who else was here on that night?' Asks Daniel.

'Lizzie is putting one together as we speak.'

'What are you betting that creepy train man pops up on that list.' Daniel grimaces in my direction.

'If you are referring to Albert Noring.' responds Fred, 'then don't waste your time, he's been checked out. The guys a freak but he's a clean freak. No previous, not even an unpaid parking ticket.'

'Who checked him out?' I ask curiously.

'New lad on the team, Jones.'

'Well I mean absolutely no offence Fred, but if it's okay with you then I'd like to speak to him again myself, maybe your new chap missed something.' Daniel does his best to sound like he isn't stepping on anyone's toes but I am not convinced it has worked.

'By all means, but the lad is good. Very keen, good observer. But, I can't stop you as you very well know. Just don't be getting caught.' He grumbles good naturedly. 'I'm running out of excuses for why you two keep popping up on my cases.'

'We won't. Trust us.' winks Daniel.

Albert Noring is today sporting beige chinos and a beige cardigan, which is gross in the fact that double beige should never be an option, but it has been made worse by the fact that he also looks beige. I feel that Albert should get out more, a little vitamin D would work wonders on his deathly pallor.

He looks less than impressed to be meeting with us once more and I say a silent prayer that my Jimmy Choos survive the horrendous ordeal that is his manky flooring.

'I don't know what you think I can tell you.' He grumbles, 'I've already spoken with the police not to mention you two. It's all rather farcical if you ask me, accusing an innocent man of kidnapping women and god knows what else. This is harassment!'

'Mr Noring... Albert...' I begin, 'Nobody has accused you of anything, we are merely gathering information that may lead us to the safe return of these ladies. Any help you give us would be greatly appreciated.' I smile, and hope that it looks genuine. 'You would like that wouldn't you Albert? To help us find these missing women?'

'Matters none to me. Find them, don't find them. How's it going to help me?'

'Because you will have done the right thing! Can you imagine how scared they must be right now? How can you even think this way?'

'And just what do you think my neighbours will be thinking right now? Those bloody curtain twitchers over the road; they'll be thinking I'm some kind of pervert that's what! All I did was try and find myself some female company, a little companionship and I get dragged into this unholy mess.'

'Rather this mess than the mess those poor women are in though, wouldn't you agree!' I snap.

Muttering under his breath, he yanks his cardigan together and motions for us to go into the living room. 'Let's just get this over and done with shall we. I have a documentary starting in twenty three minutes.'

'Albert, if you wouldn't mind, could you just set the scene for us at L.U.V on the three occasions that you were there? Any regulars? Anybody hanging around looking suspicious?' Daniel speaks calmly to Albert but I know inside he despises the man. There is no proof that he has actually committed any crime, other than that he is a soulless selfish cretin, there is no evidence to suggest that he is responsible for these missing women, but Daniel has made his mind up about him and that is that.

If we could just have him arrested based on the last few minutes of conversation with him then I would gladly call Fred and have him banged to rights.

'What can I tell you?' He shouts, throwing his arms in the air dramatically, 'I don't know anything.' Sighing he sits down in a dirty old armchair and mutes the television. 'The nights that I was there were perfectly civilised. I was a little dubious at first, thinking it would be full of scantily clad women and super model men. I was surprised to find normal people like myself, people just looking for love.'

I bite back a laugh. Normal? *Wow!*

'It was all so well organised, I tell you the manager of that place really knows her stuff. Anyway, I just followed the rules as did everybody else. A few minutes with each other, bell rings, swap over. The socialising afterwards was a little awkward for me. I mean you may not have noticed but I'm not exactly the Brad Pitt of the dating scene, and talking to the opposite sex doesn't exactly come naturally.'

'Mmm you don't say.' I reply sweetly. Daniel nudges me and urges Albert to continue.

'Well anyway, there was obviously a lot of chatter about the missing women amongst the ladies and the men were seeing this is their opportunity to be the knights in shining armour, promising all sorts of protection. Like starving sharks they were. Well what chance did I have, they were all but swooning. So I sat at the bar, had a few drinks and left. That's all that I know. Nothing happened, I didn't see anything peculiar and I know nothing other than I came home alone, as usual.'

'Did you see anybody there that you had seen previously?' Daniel asks.

'Yeah there were a few. One in particular stood out.' He laughs. 'The brightest hair I've ever seen out of a kids cartoon show. Very loud, very lively.'

'You speak to her?' I ask.

'No way.' Albert shakes his head vehemently, 'scared the living daylights out of me. She spent a lot of time talking to some of the women at the bar, never the men, so I guess she swings the other way. Each to their own I say.'

I just know that he is talking about Dendra, I mean who else would unashamedly walk around with hair brighter than a bird of paradise.

'Anybody else?'

'Just a few other women that have been before, but nobody that really stood out. Apart from the rainbow haired one.' He chuckles. 'Why can't you just check cctv in the place instead of harassing innocent people like me?' He demands, his mood changing from laughing to grumpy in a nano second.

'It's been down unfortunately. Believe me we would prefer to look at that and not bother people, but needs must.' Answers Daniel through tight lips.

'Yeah, well I've answered all of your stupid questions so you can just leave now.'

'I have one more question actually.' I smile, 'What kind of woman are you looking for at these places Albert? What is your type?'

'That's two questions and taking liberties!'

'If you wouldn't mind.'

'I'm looking for a woman. Simple. Looks? Don't care. Personality? Don't care. So long as she can cook, hold some kind of conversation and doesn't intrude on my hobby then she will be just fine.'

'And if she does intrude on your hobby?' I ask.

'Well then she better...'

'Better what?'

'I would like you to leave now, my documentary starts in three minutes.'

'A bit of a temper there Mr Noring?' Daniel directs straight at him.

'Get out!' he demands, 'get out now!'

'With pleasure.' I grimace.

Dragging her from the river my arms burn, my chest heaves. I am not strong enough. I cannot do this alone.
I pull, pull with everything that I have, pull and pray, pull and pray.
Muddy water everywhere. Everywhere.
In her eyes, her mouth, her nose. She does not breathe.
I pound desperately on her chest, thumping, thumping.
Nothing.
A breath in my ear, calm and precise.
Not panicking, not scared.
He is here, just as I feared he eventually would be.
But he does not care, he feels nothing.
A phone rings, an outgoing call.
Only time will tell now. Only time.

Chapter Twelve

It has been forty-eight hours since Daniel and I had the most interesting and bizarre conversation with Albert Noring and a lot has happened in that time.

The two missing girls from the beginning of my investigation have been found. This however is not a celebratory moment for all of those involved in the case up to press, as both of the girls are dead.

They were found by an elderly lady out walking her dogs, their poor innocent bodies dumped in some neglected farmers field on the outskirts of Wakefield.

The unusual thing about them, aside from their untimely deaths of course is that they were both wearing hospital gowns, the kind that they give you when you go in for an examination or operation, and yet neither of the girls had been operated on, thankfully.

Our lab guys have worked tirelessly over the past two days examining the gowns, dirt under their fingernails and all other manner of tests and they have they discovered something rather odd.

In the system of both girls they found traces of a drug called Burundanga. Not a normal drug by any stretch of the imagination, but John our eldest lab guy has seen this before, many years ago when he worked oversees. This particular drug originates from Columbia and the Borrachero tree, in many cases it has been documented that this drug has the power to remove free will, pretty much turning you into a human puppet.

Luckily for us Damien seems to be a bit of a pro with these

kinds of things, and I have arranged to meet with him so that he may guide us through how a person would get hold of such a thing and also what it would be used for.

Why would our kidnappers, now murderers want to remove a person's rationale? Make them suggestible to anything that they wish?

I do not know, but these maniacs have escalated from simple kidnapping to murder in record time, and I have to wonder just how much time remains for our other two missing girls?

Daniel and Fred are still adamant that Albert is somehow responsible for all of this. He never has anybody that can vouch for his whereabouts, he always claims that he was home alone watching his train documentaries, and his temper definitely leaves a lot to be desired, not to mention that we know that he was at L.U.V when the girls went missing. It really is stacking up against him.

So they have hauled him in for questioning.

ALBERT NORING

RECORDED INTERVIEW

Date:25/05/2018

Time: 10.31 am

Conducted by: Detective Frederick Gooseman

FG: This interview is being tape recorded. I am Detective Frederick Gooseman of West Yorkshire Police. What is your full name?

AN: Albert Noring. And this is absolutely ludicrous!

FG: Mr Noring if you could please hold off on the outbursts whilst I question you then this will be completed a lot quicker.

AN: I'm just saying that this...

FG: For the benefit of the tape Mr Noring please can you state your current occupation.

AN: Unemployed.

FG: So you have a lot of free time on your hands would you say?

AN: No I would not say! I am a very busy man.

FG: Busy doing what?

AN: I know what you are doing, trying to trap me. Make me muddle words so that I trip up. Well it's not gonna work.

FG: Surely if you have done nothing illegal then you wouldn't have to worry about tripping up.

AN: See there you go, making me feel like I have committed a crime.

FG: Mr Noring I am merely trying to ascertain what you do with all of your free time.

AN: I watch documentaries as you very well know.

FG: You must be pretty clued up on trains then?

AN: I know my stuff yeah, what of it?

FG: Do you put as much passion into anything else in your life as you do with your trains?

AN: No! I just like trains.

FG: Really? So you wouldn't say that finding a woman was a priority for you? Something that you would invest some serious time in?

AN: Of course it's a priority, nobody wants to be alone do they. But it's not as important as my trains.

FG: So why all of the visits to L.U.V?

AN: I just thought that I would give it a go. But it didn't work out for me.

FG: And yet you continued to go, despite not being successful, why is that?

AN: Is it a crime to try and find romance?

FG: No, but it is a crime to kidnap four women and kill two of them, that we know of.

AN: WHAT?! I haven't kidnapped or killed nobody, why are you doing this to me? Do you even have any evidence?

FG: Explain to me why when you were questioned about the missing girls from L.U.V you decided once again to go back there?

AN: I was curious okay. I figured maybe the girls would be scared, looking for a knight in shining armour to protect them, and maybe that could be me.

FG: Let me put this to you Mr Noring. I believe that you attended the first singles night at L.U.V with the full intention of meeting a woman. I believe that you approached more than one woman on that first night and they each in turn rebuffed you...

AN: No that's...

FG: Let me finish. I believe that you became so enraged with their refusal to engage with you that you did something incredibly stupid. You took one of them...

AN: No I never!

FG: I believe that you drugged this woman to make her compliant, but she was agitated wasn't she Mr Noring? You couldn't control her, so you killed her...

AN: NO!

FG: But where does that leave you now? No woman and you now have a dead body to take care of. So you keep her someplace while you grab yourself another woman, only the same happens again and you find yourself with two corpses to deal with.

But you don't panic do you Mr Noring? You just store them and forget all about them, until they begin to smell. Now you know that you have to do something.

So kidnapping your final two girls you then decide to ditch the bodies of Jemma Daines and Freya Scopes, and concentrate on your new projects.

Did you know their names Albert?

AN: This is wrong, I haven't done anything. Why would I care about their bloody names, I don't even know them! Can you even prove any of this?

FG: You know the papers are saying that the kidnapper has a thing for dolls. You have a thing for dolls Mr Noring?

AN: Dolls? What? No just my trains, just trains.

FG: Tell me a little about this temper of yours.

AN: I don't have a temper, I just don't appreciate being accused of things that I haven't done.

FG: I believe you do have a temper, and I believe that this temper of yours has gotten you into a whole heap of trouble.

AN: You don't even know me, so how would you know if I have a temper or not?

FG: I'm a Police Officer Mr Noring; it's my job to know these things.

AN: Hah! It's that bloody posh tart isn't it? Right player that one. I'll bet it's her and that action man sidekick of hers that have made up this crap about my temper. Well I don't have one. She bloody does though.

FG: Albert did you or did you not kidnap these women?

AN: For the hundredth time, no I did not.

FG: I believe that you are hiding something from me Mr Noring and I plan to get to the bottom of it.

AN: You seem to believe an awful lot detective, but tell me, do you have any proof against me?

FG: At present...

AN: No I didn't think so. If you want to speak to me again then you can do so through my solicitor. Goodbye Detective.

INTERVIEW TERMINATED AT - 11.04am

Chapter Thirteen

'I can't believe that they didn't have enough to hold him.' I grumble, 'Now he's out there again, free and raring to go.'
'I know, I know. But you can't lock somebody up for murder on account of their liking trains way too much for a normal person.' Daniel Laughs, 'Besides, Fred said that he got no vibes whatsoever from Albert, well other than him being a complete moron.'
'So where does that leave us?'
'Back to the morgue of course.' He grins manically.

'So, the Burundanga drug as you know originates from Columbia and the Borrachero tree, proper name is Scopolamine.' Damien begins in full tutor mode. 'This stuff is lethal, as you know and as you can now see.'
I try not to vomit as Damien points in the direction of Jemma Daines and Freya Scopes. They are currently laid out as respectfully as you can be when you are about to be embalmed. The coroner released the bodies after a full post-mortem had been carried out on each of the girls as he had not wanted to cause the families any further grief. The cause of death had been recorded as lethal overdose by a drug named Burundanga, Devil's Breath or Scopolamine as it is more commonly known.
'Why do you know so much about this stuff pal?' ask Daniel totally engrossed in the lesson.
'I have a lot of time on my hands.' He laughs. 'So to continue, The Burundanga drug is a whole host of badness, and I'm not just talking about being given too much of the

stuff that it kills you. The lead up to death itself via this drug is not a way that you want to go.'

'So what does it do?' I ask. 'The lab guys said that it effectively turns you into a human puppet?'

'The lab guys were right.' He sighs, 'There was a news article about this only a few months ago and how it was being used to intoxicate unsuspecting drunken revellers into handing over their holiday money, bank cards, credit cards, there were even sexual assaults.'

'How do you get hold of such a thing?' I ask, feeling nauseas.

'Believe me it's easy. Just a few clicks of your mouse and ping, delivered right to your door. It's most popular use is for curing motion sickness and nausea, but in the wrong hands this stuff is evil.'

'Side effects?' enquires Daniel.

'Well let me tell you my friend, this drug comes with a plethora of life changing nastiness. In effect if this drug is misused it can turn you into a living zombie, you will be coherent but will have zero free will, open to suggestion and it can erase your memories. The victim would literally have no idea who they are or how they came to being in such a state. It can be given via a drink or blown into the face, no matter which way this is administered it is pure evil. Doctors refer to it as 'chemical submission' on account of the victim becoming, well, submissive.'

There is silence all around the mortuary as Daniel and I take in all that has been said. How can such a thing exist?

'The questions you need to be asking guys is why would anybody want to take away a person's free will? And just what are they wanting them to become suggestible to?'

Throwing my hands in the air I lean against the door and

scream. A tad dramatic I appreciate.

'Who though?' I yell, 'we have questioned everybody. Even freaky Albert is a no go.'

'Don't forget also the hospital gowns.' Interrupts Damien, 'with the drugs and the gowns maybe you are looking for somebody that has medical training? A doctor or a nurse maybe?'

'Or maybe.' I smile, 'we are looking for somebody who has a whole range of medical equipment just lying around their back garden?'

'Dendra?' Asks Daniel.

'Well we never did get to the bottom of why she has all of that stuff out there.'

'But why would she drug anyone? I thought you were under the impression that she was only guilty of hiding a sick sister?' questions Damien, uncertain.

'Oh I don't know!' I snap. 'But it's the only avenue left available to us. Maybe she is testing the drug out before she uses it on her sister? I do not know, okay. But I am going to check this out.'

The thought that there are people out there drugging innocent folk into losing their memory is horrendous.

I know exactly what it is like to not understand, to not remember and I will not let another person suffer in this way. Sure I can't control the whole universe, but I can save Amanda Farthing and Marcy Grey.

So help me God, I will not let them die.

Chapter Fourteen

Celestia is in a delightful mood when I enter her office upon my return. Clearly this Godfrey chap is good for her, which in turn means that he is also good for me. A happy Celestia means a happy Heaven.

'You know Tiffany, I never thought that Godfrey and I would be reunited. I obviously knew that one day our paths would cross again, and I feared that day, I genuinely feared it. But to have him here, to have him back by my side has vanquished those fears. We are to be re-married, you will of course attend.'

'Interesting way of extending an invitation.' I grin, 'I would be delighted to attend.'

'You know Godfrey admitted to me that he was incredibly unhappy after I died, not just the normal mourning phase that a recently bereaved person must go through, but genuinely unhappy.

He re-married of course, believing that his continuing sadness was down to being lonely. He told me that it was the biggest mistake of his life. His new wife was not a pleasant woman by all accounts. Can you believe she actually forced him to throw all of my things away?' She shakes her head vehemently, 'Have a clear out by all means, but things that he had saved, personal things of mine? Gone! Selfish woman.

He knew not long into the marriage that he had made a monumental mistake, and try as he might to divorce her it just never came to fruition.

So the day he died was a blessing he said.

He had no idea of course that any of this existed, and was naturally shocked to discover that there is life after death. Well, a degree of it anyway. I am so happy that he is here Tiffany. I could burst. We are to throw a party, the most exquisite party that Heaven has ever seen.' She chimes merrily, 'you will of course attend.'

'Again with the personal touch.' I grumble under my breath. 'So when is this party?'

'Right after the wedding of course.'

'And that is when?' I prompt.

'Tomorrow. Why else would I be so merry?'

Smiling I nod my head and back out of the room. I have never seen Celestia so animated before.

A wedding? Tomorrow? *Okaaaay*.

Chapter Fifteen

It is raining heavily as we pull up outside of Dendra's home. The place looks quiet, but with a woman that clearly has a lot of secrets this means nothing.

I am reluctant to leave the warmth of the car and toy with the idea of begging Daniel to just go instead, but I promised myself that I would not let Amanda and Marcy die, and I am sure that if they could stand outside in the rain then they would.

I wonder if they are in there right now – Amanda and Marcy? I so desperately want to just storm in, demand answers, save the girls. But if I am wrong then Celestia will stand me up before the judges for sure, and this time I do not think even Daniel could save me. Not to mention it would totally wreck her wedding day, and I for one am not being responsible for that. Angry Celestia in a bridal gown? *No thanks!*

As Daniel raps loudly on the front door I peer around for any signs of movement, the place is eerily quiet, even the birds do not sing today.

'What?' Snaps Stella, swinging open the door, 'she's not here and I've nowt to say to either of you.'

'Stella, please.' I soothe, 'we just want to help.'

'Help what? There's nothing here that we need your help with.'

'I know that Dendra needs helps.'

'Oh yeah? And how'd you know that then?'

'Why are you standing in our way?' demands Daniel, 'you know that your friend cannot continue along the way she is doing, she needs professional guidance, why can't you see that?'

'Is that right? And just what do you think she needs professional guidance with?' Stella snaps.

'With her sick sister of course.' I smile. 'We can help. At the very least we can put you both in touch with organisations that can help. What do you say?'

'I say that I'd like to know just what the hell you are on about? Aint nobody sick in here.'

Stella looks old today. Definitely a lot older than she looked the previous time that we visited. She looks more grey somehow. I wonder if she feels pale in comparison to the bright and vivacious Dendra?

I wonder what her role in all of this is and if she truly wants the part that she has been given.

Dendra seems to me to be the life and soul of the party, and Stella just the little wallflower. How did they even meet, what do they even have in common?

Her jeans are stained; as is her t-shirt and I just know that she could vastly improve if she sought help. I'm not talking like full blown super model here, but a wash with soap wouldn't do her any harm.

'We know all about her Stella, and we just want to give you some support, to let both yourself and Dendra know that you are not alone.'

'You know nothing!' she spits.

'We know all about the medical supplies. The feeding tubes alone have given the game away. Do you not feel that she deserves more than this?' I wave my arms to the side of me, 'would a private hospital not be a much better place for her?'

She laughs and it strangely reminds me of a crow, 'Private

hospital? Are you crazy? Does it look to you like we even have a pot to piss in?'

'There's no need to be vulgar, I was merely suggesting...'

'I'll tell you what princess, you get me the brass needed to put Bronwyn in a private hospital and I'll take her there myself!'

'Bronwyn?' Daniel quizzes.

Stella realises much too late that she has made a monumental error and tries to backtrack. 'Bronwyn what?' she asks nonchalantly.

'You said Bronwyn?'

'No I didn't, you must be off your damn heads.'

'Why don't you just tell us what is really going on here Stella, all we want to do is help?' I whisper.

Somewhere inside this disgusting hovel of a home is a girl that desperately needs our assistance and we can't get past the bloody pit-bull on the front door.

'Get lost!' she screams in our faces, 'If I see you round here again I'll get my gun and screw the consequences.'

Slamming the door in our faces we stand and digest this new information. She does have a sister; we had suspected this to be the case, but why oh why is she being hidden away?

And why no matter how many people we question do we always end up coming back here?

What happened to this girl?

Why is she some big dirty secret?

Re-hashing the evidence up to press I know that I have to make a suggestion to Daniel that is going to make him crazy. More than likely he will put his foot down and outright refuse, but the logic remains the same whether he likes it or not. We need help.

We need to know how crazy, unbalanced, socially retarded people think.
We need the Devil.

Chapter Sixteen

The party is in full swing with everybody drinking celebratory toasts to the happy couple.
Celestia looked absolutely stunning as she floated down the aisle, like seriously she floated, must be some crazy Queen of Heaven stuff going on there.
Her dress was simple yet chic, a plain white gown with a tiny train studded with diamonds; I am inclined to believe that they will have been real diamonds.
Now though she is wearing a pale blue dress and matching sandals as Godfrey twirls her around the dance floor.
I asked her why she had taken the gown off, she laughed and told me that when they were first married she could not afford a wedding dress, and her wearing one today was all just part of fulfilling some silly little girls dream. That she felt like a princess for the moment that it mattered, but now it was time to become a wife.
Not actually one hundred percent sure what that even means, but she looks happy and it seems to make sense to her.
Victoria is spinning Sophie and Maisie around and around and their giggles echo through the room, so happy, so content.
Daniel as always looks divine in his tuxedo, like a casual James Bond... I say this because he is still wearing his sneakers. No matter what I said he just would not part with them.
I am wearing a pink floor length gown from Vera Wang with matching Jimmy Choos and I have to say that I look a

million dollars. *Obviously.*

'Hey Tiff, get your butt over here and bring me another drink.' Shouts Tracey who is already looking a little worse for wear.

'Don't you think you've had enough.' I laugh, naughtily handing her another glass of champagne.

'Nah!' she giggles hysterically, 'Now listen.' She attempts to whisper but fails miserably, 'Victoria and I were planning your hen, so tell me.' She hiccups, 'you wanna posh do like this or what?'

'Hey hush up you.' Scolds Victoria, 'The hen is not supposed to know a thing about our plans.'

'Oh yeah, my bad.'

'I will be happy with whatever you choose ladies.' I smile. *Please God let it be classy, I pray.*

'Right well I'm off to boogie, laters.' Shouts Tracey as she stumbles towards the dance floor.

'Wow, she's sure had a few.' Victoria raises her eyebrows in mock disapproval.

'Yep. There will be a few sore heads in the morning I should imagine.' As silence falls between us I decide to take the plunge and ask Victoria something that has been playing on my mind for a little while.

'Do you have your wings yet?'

'Nope.' She sighs, 'I really want them too, sounds like they would be a neat accessory to have on account of our being angels.'

'Mmm me neither, I wonder why that is?' I muse.

'Dunno, some of the girls said they arrive when you prove yourself, some say it's during a big happy event that you go through. I guess only time will tell.'

'Maybe when Daniel and I are married? I know that we

can't have children; I have come to terms with that I think. So maybe when we are married I will become a true angel and I won't just be winging it.'

Chapter Seventeen

'Like hell!' Shouts Daniel, 'Not happening, no way.'
We are currently standing outside of a cafe with the intention of buying proper coffee, not that instant stuff that Daniel normally drinks and he has erupted like a crazed volcano. People are staring which does not seem to bother him, but I Tiffany Delamarre shall not be made a spectacle of.
Dragging him into an alleyway which disgustingly smells of urine, I look around to ensure that we are alone.
'Look, it was just a suggestion; I'm not trying to force you into anything.' I try to calm him down, unsuccessfully.
'Let me get this straight...' He's pacing now, not a good sign, 'You want me to take the woman that I love into the fiery pits of Hell? Satan's Lair? And have a nice cosy little chat with the Devil while he flirts shamelessly with my wife to be? Does that sound about right?'
'You have no need to be jealous...'
'Jealous?! The guy is a bloody maniac. Not happening Tiff, not a chance.'
'I just thought that he might be able to point us in the direction of our killer, on account of him being mental. He kind of knows these things.'
'Yes Tiffany, he knows them because he is the King of all evil.'
'Okay, okay, just forget that I said anything.' I sigh.
'Fighting over me? How wonderful.' Lucifer drawls, 'But really there is no need, for here I am.'
The Devil as always looks devastatingly gorgeous, and if I

were a crazed denizen of Hell then I would certainly be tempted. But I am not, and I am very much engaged.

Throwing myself in front of Daniel I plead with him not to do anything crazy.

'Get the hell out of here.' He yells, 'We don't need help from the likes of you.'

'Oh but I feel that you do. You see, you are so far off track that I am certain you will never find your way back again. There is a killer out there you know.'

'Of course we bloody know!'

'Guys, guys please.' I soothe, 'this need not get ugly.' Placing my hand into Daniel's, I face Lucifer head on and ask him outright to help us.

'Tell me dear Tiffany, did you read the book of lies yet?'

'The Bible is not full of lies, you just disagree with it because you cannot bend it to fit in with your own created rules.'

'Humour me please, read it.'

'We need your help.' I begin, quickly changing the 'we' to 'I' at the scowl on Daniel's face. 'There is a killer...'

'Isn't there always.' He sniggers.

'You're not helping!'

'I wasn't aware that I had agreed to.'

'For crying out loud this is ridiculous! Stop entertaining him Tiffany, he's just playing with you.'

'Let me assure you Mr Fox that I never just play'

'Oh yeah? And what the hell is that supposed to mean?'

'Just pointing out your mistake. Easily made. Let me show you my home Daniel, I am sure that you will be most agreeable with it.'

'No thanks.'

'Tiffany, you will accompany me?'

'Not on your life is she going anywhere with you! Understand?'

'Juliana misses you... she screams her love.'

'Stop okay!'I hiss, 'bringing Juliana into this is uncalled for. Don't you dare try and make me feel guilty about her; she deserves to be where she is, like all of the other child killers that you collect! Now I need your help, so either help me or get lost!'

'Feisty, I like that. Tell me what you require and I will see if I can help you. But remember what I said the last time we met Tiffany... never forget that.'

Ignoring Daniel's look of utter confusion I put Lucifer's comment to the back of my mind and remind myself to explain all to Daniel later.

How could I ever forget him in my bathroom whilst I was bathing, telling me with absolute confidence that I would one day be his. *Hardly!*

'Four women have been kidnapped, only now two of those four are dead, found wearing hospital gowns. We have interviewed everybody that could potentially be involved and we are no further in cracking the case.

We interviewed a man who goes by the name of the 'Dreamcatcher', he said that he has had dreams of the missing girls. We then find out that the girls were drugged with something called Burundanga, but also goes by the name of 'Devil's Breath' Which made me think you had something to do with it...'

'Charmed I'm sure.' He smirks.

'...So I now think that maybe the Dreamcatcher has more to do with this than he is letting on, and these dreams of his are just part of some elaborate game that he is playing with us. Much like you do.'

'I am hurt Tiffany that you would think so little of me. Did I not help you on your last case? Did I not lead you to where you needed to be?'

'You led me on a merry dance is what you did! Do not think for one moment that I have forgotten what happened to Kimberley when you burnt the spa to the ground!'

'Ah yes, that was unfortunate.' He grins, 'But still, the case was cracked, was it not?'

'Unfortunate?! You left her to burn alive!' I yell.

'There are always casualties in war dear Tiffany.'

'It was not a war.'

'If I bother you so, if my methods are insane to you, then why do you always seek me out?'

'Because our killer is nuts and so are you?' I answer sweetly.

'Quite.' He laughs.' So, tell me more about this Dreamer.'

'The police have checked him out thoroughly. He's squeaky clean.'

'So you accuse the man based on his dreams? Do you not dream Tiffany? Tell me what you dream.'

Ignoring his questions I plough straight on, 'There is a woman that we are looking into, Dendra, she has a sick sister that she is hiding away, so would have access to medical supplies, hospital gowns that sort of thing, but why would she kidnap and drug other women? Nothing adds up – which is why I need your assistance.'

'Tell me, why have you not simply broken into this Dendra's place of residence? Surely then you would have the answers that you seek?'

'Because her crazed housemate has a shot gun!'

'Oh I see. Worried that you will be killed twice are you?' He mocks.

'Well of course not.' I lie, though the thought had entered my head when she mentioned a gun, stupidly.

'Then what are you waiting for?'

'Is that it? All of these infuriating little mind games and you tell me to just break in? I thought you had more about you than that.'

As Daniel holds the door of the cafe open for me I look back once more at the Devil, he has a strange look on his face, twisted.

'Never doubt me Tiffany, I will tell you one thing if only to have you believe that I do have more about me... As you will one day learn. There is a person out there dreaming, terrifying, torturous dreams, and this person is linked closely to your investigation. But it is not poor old Leonard Critchin. He knows nothing.'

'How did you...?' I begin.

'Know his name? My dearest Tiffany, I know everything. Ask and it will be given to you, seek and you will find, knock and the door will be opened to you, blah blah blah! See you around.' He winks.

'What an absolute crack-pot he is!' snaps Daniel.

Sitting down in the warm cafe Daniel orders our coffees and eventually the scowl leaves his handsome face. But I am left wondering...

Did Lucifer just quote the Bible at me?

Blue lights fill the night sky, flashing and offering some ray of hope. Still he stands unmoving, he does not help, he does not speak.

Questions over and over, the woman with the radio repeats her words, I hear nothing, I hear nothing but the sirens, see nothing but the blue.

Clinical, clean - the dirt has gone but the situation remains the same, still no life, still no breath, still no words.

How can he be this still, this calm, this unfeeling.

More questions, I shake my head, the tears taking over once more.

They sedate me, I am falling under, maybe I will die too, maybe this is my punishment.

As I close my eyes I see him, and still he does not move.

Chapter Eighteen

We have waited patiently in the back of Damien's van for all sign of life to leave Dendra's residence. It has been a tense few hours, not to mention cold and stinky. Seriously the back of this private ambulance smells a little sketchy.

Damien has come along purely for the thrill of the chase but also in case Amanda and Marcy are in there, that way he can whisk them away to be seen to, by the hospital obviously, not him. Hopefully.

Daniel called Fred on the way over, he was unable to attend as his presence was unfortunately required at another crime scene, but assured us that he would head over our way just as soon as he was able, and to contact 999 should we find ourselves in any trouble.

I hope that we do not.

Daniel once again has his trusty toolkit and with no effort at all we are inside the property.

The air smells dirty, yet sanitized at the same time, and I immediately begin my search of the rooms on the ground floor.

If I was a badass kidnapper / killer/ deranged nurse then where would I hide my victims and sick sister?

'Heading to the basement Tiff, you okay up here or are you coming with me?' Yells out Daniel, making me jump.

There is no way that I'm wondering around this place by myself, so I run to his side as we locate the door to the room below the house.

Damien has stayed outside to keep a look out and to be immediately on hand should anyone need driving quickly to the emergency services.

Beeping greets us as Daniel pushes open the basement door, I at first think that we have set off some kind of alarm until Daniel flicks on the lights.

There in the centre of the room lays Bronwyn.

She is attached to so many wires and tubes that it is impossible to see where she begins and the machines end.

'Oh My God!' I gasp, running to her bedside, 'Oh Daniel, she needs help. We have to help her.'

Pulling me away from the lifeless form on the bed Daniel makes me see sense. Right now she is okay, but Amanda and Marcy may still need us.

Not caring about being quiet now I feel rage burning deep inside of me as I yell out for Amanda and Marcy.

Nothing. Silence.

Taking a deep breath I look around the horrible stainless steel room and wonder what on earth could have possessed Dendra to keep her sister this way.

What was she thinking?

'Tiff, over here.' Shouts Daniel, 'I've found them.'

In a dark little room no larger than a closet where you may keep your coats and wellington boots sits Amanda Farthing, the closet beside it is exactly the same, only that one has Marcy Grey tucked away inside.

The Dreamcatcher was right.

Everything that Leonard said was correct -

The room, the air vents, the vivid colours, which must surely be Dendra's wigs – the beeping, oh my god, he was right about everything.

The women are both exactly like Damien said they would be too. Zombies. I have never seen anything like it.

Their lips are so parched that they have begun to crack and

peel, hair hangs limp and dirty around their pale faces and their eyes are so sunken and blank. Like dolls eyes.

Calling Damien I ask him to come down to the basement to help Daniel carry the girls out.

I had imagined that we would find them and they would be weak, but they would smile somehow, relieved to be found.

I had not imagined that they would be lifeless. Had I not heard the shallow breathing for myself I would have assumed they were dead.

Wiping tears from my eyes I make my way over to Bronwyn's bed.

I hope Dendra arrives real soon, because I have a few choice words for her.

I am now one pissed off Angel!

Chapter Nineteen

'Well I said if you don't give me a good deal on the catheters then I'll take my trade elsewhere.'
We listen as Stella's voice booms though the house, and Dendra mutters none interested responses.
Damien has taken Amanda and Marcy to the hospital, but I don't feel that it's looking good for them. How are they going to recover from this ordeal?
Will they ever remember who they truly are after all of the brainwashing and drugs?
Daniel has taken Stella's gun from the porch and checked everywhere else that he could that there was not another one knocking around.
It is not for our safety clearly, but the safety of Bronwyn. If Dendra feels that that Bronwyn is threatened and her secret is out then she may do something drastic.
'Why have you left the basement open, idiot!' Screeches Dendra.
'I never. I locked it up real tight as always.'
'Then get down there and have a look! I swear if those bleedin' kids have been down there!'
I will never for as long as I am deceased forget the look on not only Stella's face, but also Dendra's face when they entered the basement.
I suppose seeing me holding the plug to her beloved sister's life support wouldn't have helped the shock much.
'Put that down, now!' she screams whilst lunging towards me.
Daniel however quick as an arrow steps out from the

torture closet, shotgun in hand.

'I suggest you all calm yourselves down and back up towards that wall there. Go.'

'That's my bloody gun.' Snaps Stella, angrily.

'Not anymore it isn't – now why don't you do us all a favour and start talking.' He commands.

Stella begins to shake, finally realising that this sick game has reached its conclusion.

'Tell 'em Dendra, there's nothing we can do now. It's over.' She cries.

'Shut your goddamn mouth and let me think.'

'No. The time for thinking has well and truly passed.' I laugh without humour, 'Had you been thinking then your poor sister would be being looked after properly. Had you been thinking Jemma Daines and Freya Scopes would still be alive. Had you been thinking Amanda farthing and Marcy Grey would not have had their lives destroyed. So less of the thinking and more of the talking, or I pull the plug.'

'Don't you dare touch her!'

'Speak or she slips away peacefully.'

'Why? You wouldn't understand.' She sobs. Her tears are wasted on me, I feel nothing.

'Try me.'

'Just tell 'em D.' Urges Stella, 'It's over now.'

Dendra has a look of pure fear upon her face, gone is the bright bubbly woman from before all of this, now she looks drab, out of place. Pathetic.

'Bronwyn tried you know, to get Father to like her. But nothing that she did was ever good enough really. I think he enjoyed berating her, making her feel useless. Our Mother was a drug addict, it killed her eventually, but I suppose she brought it upon herself.

For some reason Father liked me, I could do no wrong, and even though I knew that the way he was treating Bronwyn was unkind I did nothing to help her. I didn't want him to hate me too.

He would pinch her and prod her until she cried out in pain and I did nothing, in fact I helped. I would do anything to make Father like me.

The night that she ran away was the worst night of my whole life. I still have nightmares about it now. Every single night of my life, on loop, the same terrifying nightmares.'

Leonard saw these too! I remember. God he's good!

'I chased her and now in hindsight she must have thought that Father had sent me to bring her back. She must have been so scared, so fearful of the punishment that he would give her.

It was raining heavily that night, I saw her fall a few times, but the last time she fell she did not get back up. The river was so angry that night. She fell in and she didn't move again. I pulled her out and prayed for her to breathe, but she struggled. I remember him standing over me. Not once did he care, worry or grieve. He was like a statue.

The paramedics got her heart beating again, but she would never again open her eyes. Her heart was broken, so what was the point in her trying.

Over the years I watched as Father moved Bronwyn from one expensive medical centre to the next. Eventually when the pressure was off of him, when he no longer felt like he had to pretend to care he had her moved back home. Shoved in some backroom out of the way. I knew then that I had a choice to make.

Leave her with him forever or bring her here and look after her myself. Maybe make up for the lost years where I stupidly didn't defend her.

I found Stella on the streets, paid her a nice sum to help me, an offer she couldn't refuse really, help me and I will share my home, she's been here ever since – helping me.'

'Don't treat her very well though do you' I snap.

'No. No, you're right, I don't and for that I am sorry.'

'Okay so you have her home, now what?'

'I planned to care for her, to bring her back to life, but the more I tried the more I knew that her body and her brain were just not working anymore. They had finally given up. So I had a plan.'

'I'm guessing this is where the kidnapped women come into it?' I ask.

She continues, ignoring my question. 'My plan was so simple and so perfect. I would find women that were the same height, weight, eyes and hair colour of my sister and I would brainwash them into thinking they were her.' She sounds excited now and I am a little freaked out. 'I would drug them over a course of months and play voice recordings, stories of our past through the air vents convincing them that they were Bronwyn. Eventually they would believe that they were.'

'Interesting. Only Bronwyn's past wasn't that rosy was it? You made out to me that sister's were the best of friends, someone that you could always rely on, you even said that having friends wasn't the same as having a sister. You can't even tell the truth to yourself can you? Have you lied to yourself every single day that she has been here, that your relationship was perfect? That your childhood was idyllic? *Really?*'

'I made some stuff up, those drugs, well they make you believe anything anyway, and it's not like she ever would have known the truth.'

'But it all went wrong didn't it? With Jemma and Freya?'

'I used too much okay, got a little carried away with myself and blew too much in through the vents. Next thing I know they've overdosed and I'm back to square one.'

'Oh what a shame.' I sigh sarcastically.

'It was actually, yes.'

'So tell me, if the brainwashing had been a success how were you going to get past the fact that none of the girls you kidnapped bore even a slight facial resemblance to Bronwyn? Were you just going to ignore that fact? Who cares, you have a semi new sister so you can get rid of the old one now?'

'This is why she went off you.' Whispers Stella. 'Because your eyes weren't right.'

'Excuse me?'

'I planned rather cleverly I feel to put Bronwyn's face onto the successful patient, thus creating a brand new version of my beautiful innocent sister.'

'Holy shit!' Daniels voice startles me.

'Sorry, what? You planned to swap their faces? What in god's name is wrong with you?'

'It is a perfectly legitimate plan.' She huffs sulkily.

'Aside from the fact that you are completely nuts, have you ever seen a face transplant? They never look like the person they took the face from because our faces are all different shapes and sizes. How were you even going to do this? Did you watch some tutorials on YouTube? Watch Frankenstein movies? I'm at a loss here, explain!'

'I have self taught myself over the years; surgery really

isn't that difficult once you know the basics. It would have worked out fine until you two started poking your noses in. Now it is all ruined. Poor Bronwyn will be shipped away to some medical facility, they may even switch off the machines, and it's all down to you!'

'No. It's all down to you. You and your selfishness. Bronwyn has always deserved better than you! Maybe now she will finally get it.'

Just as I finish my rant the machine that has been keeping Bronwyn alive for all of these years begins to beep. I hear Dendra screaming, see Daniel holding her back. But I care not for her.

Bending down to Bronwyn's ear I whisper softly to her, 'see you on the other side sweet angel' and then she is gone. I know that I will see her again, of course I will, because she is free now.

R.I.P.

Bronwyn

It was always the same for me, no matter what I said, no matter what I did she was always the golden girl. I was always the ugly, stupid unwanted one.

I tried really I did. I cooked and cleaned, made the beds, washed the windows but still it was never good enough for them.

I believed for a long time that I truly was useless, just like they said. But laying here all alone with only her voice for company I realised how very wrong they were. How what they were doing to me was abusive and unkind. They were the horrible ones, not me.

I put up with everything that they dished out to me, the spitting in my food, pulling my ponytail so hard that I cried out in pain. I knew that I would never be a proper part of the family, I knew that I wasn't loved, but what hurt most of all was the way my own sister hurt me, the way she would do things just to please her Father, so that he wouldn't turn his attention to her.

I call him her Father because he was never a Father to me. No Father would hurt and humiliate his child the way he did to me daily. I never had a Father.

I don't know why I wasn't wanted. Mother was an insignificant part of my life; she always seemed to be in some kind of a trance. I think maybe now she was a drug user, it matters none. She never once lifted a finger to help me or speak out for me, so for that I do not class her as anything. She is nothing to me.

The night I ran away I was so incredibly scared. Would

they chase me and drag me back, punish me further for daring to be so insolent.

I had this fantasy that I would live out in the woods with the furry animals, I would learn how to communicate with them and they would take me in as one of their own. Stupid I know, but when you have nothing you will grab at anything, no matter how unrealistic.

The rain was horrendous that night, crazily I had not formed an actual plan of action and I just ran barefoot into the woods in only my night dress, I was soaked by the time I reached the trees, but I was determined, oh so determined. They were not going to catch me, I wouldn't allow it.

Her voice echoing through the night only made me more insistent on disappearing. He will have sent her out looking for me. I knew then that my punishment would be harsh. So I ran, I ran until my feet were sore and bloody, my arms scratched raw on the brambles.

I didn't see the drop until it was too late, had not noticed how swollen the river was with the torrential downpour. I felt myself slipping and all I could think was thank you, thank you for letting me escape, thank you for taking me away from this pain.

When I awoke, well in my mind anyway, I soon learnt that I was completely paralysed from head to toe and I could not speak. But inside I was still me, I could still think and feel and hear and I knew once more that I was trapped. I would never be free.

The years passed in a blur of nurses, doctors, tests, and me praying for the day to arrive when they would just pull the plug. That day never came.

I heard Dendra apologising over and over, begging for

forgiveness. Had I been able to speak I would have told her that I could never forgive her, and how I wish that she was the one in this bed, not me. She deserved no life.

I know that she took me from his home, maybe her last chance to salvage something of her barely there conscience, but it meant nothing other than being under her control once more.

I prayed, oh how I prayed, please God if you are listening, send an angel to save me so that I may be free of this torment, this degrading shame, save me from her, I beg of you.

Feeling sleepy for the first time in a long time, I closed my eyes and I knew, I just knew that I was finally free, for I had heard the voice of angel.

Chapter Twenty

All is well that ends well it would seem.

I can fully understand and relate to Dendra's desperate need to repent and salvage something from the way she treated her sister. The desire to make things right over ruled all of her rational thinking, turning her into a woman possessed and almost obsessed with being forgiven.

Yes, I understand. I too have been the cause of creating such heinous emotions in people, I too hurt and abused and ridiculed. But I have never wanted to remove somebody's face like that freak in the Texas Chainsaw Massacre and stitch it onto someone else's fleshless chops.

Seriously! It is one thing desiring forgiveness, but it is quite another to maim and destroy in the pursuit of it.

Dendra for her own safety I would say, and that of every woman who even bears a slight resemblance to Bronwyn is now locked securely away in a padded room where she cannot harm another soul or herself. How she screamed when she was arrested, it was horrendous to hear in all honesty. I know that she can never be forgiven for the atrocities that she has caused, but somewhere there has to be some sympathy. After fighting for so long to bring her sister back, albeit in a seriously deranged way, and then watching her slip away has to be difficult. To know that she is now truly alone in this world. It's sad really.

It was odd the way that Bronwyn just slipped away like that. I fully plan to catch up with her when she gets through the queue and ask her if she was aware of what was going on around her, or if all of these years have been black and noiseless. I pray for her sake that she knew nothing; I pray that she just fell asleep the night of the accident and never felt pain again.

Dendra assured Daniel and I that Bronwyn was not brain dead, that she knew, that she could hear. I hope it was all lies, that she was wrong.

Stella the complete loon was pathetically released without charge after claiming Dendra had brainwashed her also. She must however attend weekly psyche evaluations and I fully intend to ensure that she does. Fred was understandably frustrated and angered with the decision to let her go, but when the powers that be speak all of the little minions must obey.

The two women that Daniel and I rescued, Amanda and Marcy are back home now slowly recovering from their ordeals. I hope that any damage caused by Dendra and Stella can be reversed, and that they do not go through life believing in some small way that they are in fact related to that wacko.

When questioned about the nights that they were kidnapped Amanda and Marcy were unfortunately very vague. The drug that had been administered to them was still at that point very much in their systems and we were informed that it would be a while before they were able to truly say what happened. If at all.

It has been a harrowing case that has proven to me that grief, absolution and guilt can be a rather deadly combination if not dealt with correctly.

Had Dendra just reached out then maybe all of this could have been avoided.

But she did not, so now she must face the unavoidable. Her conscience.

I have a new case now. I was going to take some time off, plan the wedding, and relax. But this last investigation has been an emotional one and I feel a brand new mystery will help me move on from it. The only problem is, this new case centres around dead people, and I am fully aware that I shouldn't be scared by that or nervous on account of the fact that I am very much dead myself, but these are like real dead people, like actual dead bodies.

Damien has a problem *(well a few actually)* and he needs my help much to his dismay. I am sure Daniel or some other angel would have been preferable, but he's stuck with me. Lucky guy.

So, basically the gist of it is this:-

Damien is a fully qualified embalmer and tutor and he takes on students, teaching them how to become just as freaky deaky as he is, which in some messed up way is fine, but at least one of these new students is up to no good.

You see Damien has found additional body parts inside of his coffins, coffins that he assures me have only ever housed one human being. The odd leg here, an extra arm or two there is so not conducive to good business practice and he understandably wants the culprit caught ASAP.

The police are not aware, apart from Fred of course, on account of the fact that should word get out that Damien Kernick runs a funeral home where you may be burying or cremating more than just your loved one it would be game over. Business closed.

He didn't mention this problem to us out of respect for our current investigation and because he knew that he was next in line for our assistance.

Currently he has the additional body parts frozen, god

knows where, hopefully not next to his peas and McCain oven chips. They are to be returned to their rightful owner when all of this has been figured out - at that point we are going to be relying heavily on Fred to keep the lid on as much of this as he can. The newspapers would have a field day with this madness.

He believes it to be one of his new embalming students, but proof is thin on the ground and catching them via cctv has proved fruitless. This is where I come in.

I am going undercover as a student...

An embalming student...

BARF!

Printed in Poland
by Amazon Fulfillment
Poland Sp. z o.o., Wrocław